MW01631690

# SEARCHING FOR WINSLET (SPECIAL FORCES: OPERATION ALPHA)

FALLPORT RESCUE OPERATIONS
BOOK FIVE

JEN TALTY

Dear Readers,

*Welcome to the Special Forces: Operation Alpha Fan-Fiction world!*

If you are new to this amazing world, in a nutshell the author wrote a story using one or more of my characters in it. Sometimes that character has a major role in the story, and other times they are only mentioned briefly. This is perfectly legal and allowable because they are going through Aces Press to publish the story.

This book is entirely the work of the author who wrote it. While I might have assisted with brainstorming and other ideas about which of my characters to use, I didn't have any part in the process or writing or editing the story.

I'm proud and excited that so many authors loved my characters enough that they wanted to write them into their own story. Thank you for supporting them, and me!

READ ON!

Xoxo
Susan Stoker

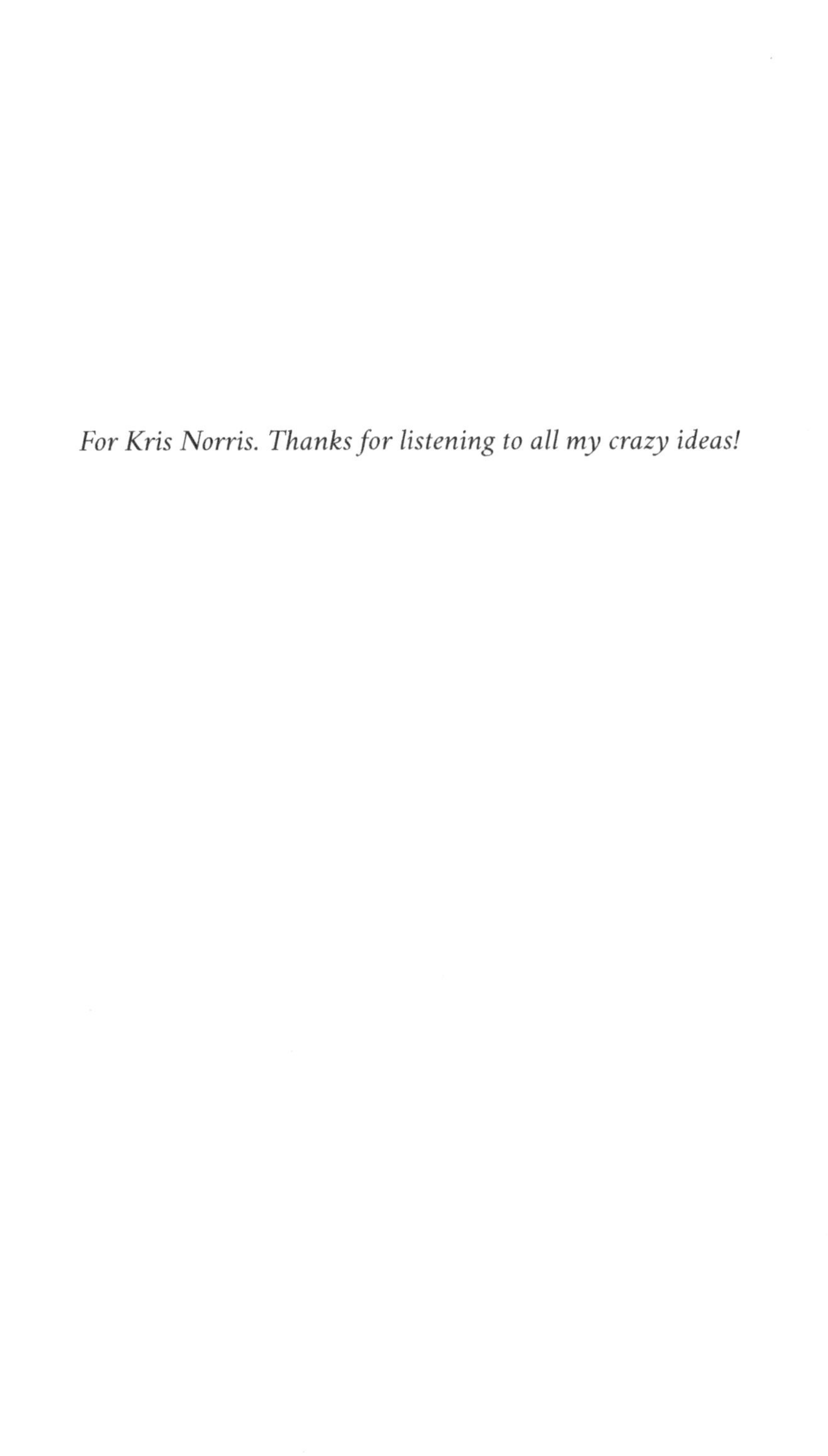

*For Kris Norris. Thanks for listening to all my crazy ideas!*

# CHAPTER ONE

Jett McCoy didn't think there were too many things in life worth complaining about. In middle school, he'd been cut from the modified soccer team, which meant there was no way in hell he was making the freshman team, much less JV or varsity.

Lucky for him, he had two passions when it came to sports. While being a golfer wasn't as appealing to the ladies, it gave him a place for quiet introspection, something he desperately needed more than a space for exerting energy as a teenager.

Golf had given Jett more than a team to letter in. It also came with recruitment to some of the best colleges. The most unlikely candidate: West Point Military Academy. So, really, in the long run, losing soccer wasn't anything to complain about.

Jett glanced in the side-view mirror before pulling into a parking spot near On The Rocks, a restaurant and bar owned by an old Army buddy. Jett and Zeke had worked together for two years before Zeke had done the unthinkable and left the military for greener pastures.

If there even was such a thing.

Now Zeke had a wife and five freaking kids. One in college and four under the age of seven. Insanity is what that was.

It was not that Jett was complaining about life because he wasn't, but this wasn't how he was supposed to go out. He had at least nine more good years of active duty. Sure, he was forty-one years old, and perhaps he would have had to pull back on the special ops missions. Do more planning and training than running in like he was the star of a *Mission Impossible* movie. He got that people aged. He understood that everyone was punching a time clock.

But to be told he could no longer serve his country except for behind a desk? He rubbed his knees and shifted in his seat. He had more metal in his body than anyone else he knew, including his grandmother, who proudly called herself the bionic woman.

He chuckled at that thought.

Again, not really complaining.

He was vertical. And it was his choice to leave the Army. He could have stayed. He could have taken that desk job, and it was an important one. But after his fourth or fifth surgery, Jett had become bitter. Hardened.

And he was done.

Kind of like when he watched his wife walk out the door.

Though, even Jett could admit that failed marriage was mostly his fault. Back then, it was his career he'd been married to anyway. It had been all that mattered to him. All that had been important since he stepped foot on West Point.

Now, everything had changed, and Jett didn't know who he was or what to do next. The only thing he knew for sure was that he'd made the right decision by retiring.

He shut down the engine of his truck and eased from behind the steering wheel. The spring evening air smacked his skin. Having grown up in Western, New York, this time of year, the temperatures could be anywhere from forty to sixty during the nighttime hours. But humid? Hell no. Where he was from, summer only happened for two weeks in July, and in April, it could snow.

It was April.

It should be cold.

He shouldn't want to lift his shirt and wipe his brow.

It amazed most that he'd become a scratch golfer by the age of fourteen, living in the part of the state that snowed starting in October most years. But for as good as he was at golf, he used to be that good of a downhill skier.

Those days were over.

At least he could still chase the white ball around the green fairways.

That was something.

He rubbed the back of his neck as he made his way toward the bar. When Zeke had heard about Jett's near-death experience, Zeke had been on the first plane. He sat with Jett. For weeks. For longer than any other human outside of his family.

Including his girlfriend at the time, but Jett couldn't blame her, not really.

Before Zeke had even gotten there, Jett had gone through a heart procedure to repair damage from shrapnel that had nicked one chamber of his heart. He had to have five of his ribs plated. And had been on a ventilator for six days because both lungs had been punctured. There were some other issues, but Jett didn't like to dwell on the fact that no one thought he would make it.

That had been sixteen months ago. Since then, Jett had three surgeries to correct issues with his heart. A hip and two knee replacements because his had been broken so badly they wouldn't heal properly. And both his shoulders had undergone surgeries to repair damage done by either bullets tearing through his body or pieces of a helicopter landing on it.

If there was ever a time to complain, it would have been during the first eight months after the helicopter went down. Or during the hell that was called rehab.

But no. Jett wasn't going to give death the last laugh. He beat death. Cheated it out of its victory.

More than once.

Only now, Jett was a shell of a man and all he wanted to do was bitch about it.

However, his grandma would find him and smack the back of his head. So, it was not worth it.

He locked his SUV and strolled across the street. Fallport, Virginia, seemed like a quaint little town. It felt like a cross between the Midwest and the South.

Or perhaps West Virginia, which was a land all by itself.

It was a good place to find out what kind of man Jett would become in this second chapter of his life.

He glanced at his watch. A little after seven. Perfect time for a cheeseburger, fries, and tall beer. He pushed open the door and scanned the room, making mental notes of everyone—and everything. Old habits died hard, and he figured this would never go away. He rubbed the center of his chest as he weaved through the room, dodging a few of the patrons who stood in the middle of the bar, conversing while their bodies swayed with the country music that filled the air.

"Look what the cat finally dragged in." Zeke waved from behind the bar. "I thought you were going to be here a couple of hours ago." He leaned in for a bro hug.

"I made a few extra stops along the way."

"Well, it worked out for the best." Zeke slapped his shoulder. "A few of the guys from Search and Rescue are here. Let me introduce you since you'll end up seeing a lot of them working for parks and recreation."

Jett had lucked out big-time when Zeke sent him the information regarding the ranger position. Jett worried he wouldn't get the job, but thanks to a few letters of recommendation, he'd been offered the position three weeks ago and he pounced on it without hesitation.

Moving away from his family would be a big change. He'd come to rely on them heavily over the last few months. However, it was time for a fresh start. Time for Jett to pick up the pieces of his mangled life and move on.

He followed Zeke through the packed bar, turning his head as he passed a table of four women. After his divorce, his dating record had gone back to what it looked like when he'd first joined the Army.

A string of meaningless short-lived relationships that meant nothing.

That was until the crash. Of course, when that happened, he'd been dating one lady who had struck his fancy a little more than most had. She was sweet. Kind. Generous. Intelligent. A woman who more than warmed his bed at night. A woman he'd gotten used to and one he could see perhaps going the distance with.

He'd cared about Becky. He'd even thought about asking her to move in with him after this last deployment. But his injuries had scared the shit out her and while she sat at his bedside for the next six months, she didn't have it in her to stay with him for the long haul.

He couldn't blame her. He was lucky to walk out of that hospital.

His gaze caught one of the girls. She had long reddish hair that bounced over her shoulders like a shampoo commercial. Her eyes were the color of an emerald. And her smile sucker punched him in the gut.

Damn.

"That's Winslet Payne. Our local forensic anthropologist." Zeke chuckled.

"I wasn't looking, much less asking," Jett said. "Although, now that you brought it up, I have to ask. What does a small town like Fallport need with a forensic anthropologist?" He honestly didn't need to know and he sure as hell shouldn't have asked. He was a man destined for trouble when it came to women.

"Do you even know what that kind of doctor does?" Zeke paused, arching his brow.

"They study old dead bones." Zeke shook his head. "You forget, I was a combat medic. I might not be a doctor, but I'm not an idiot and I patched you up a time or two in the field."

"My wife is still pissed at how this scar looks." Zeke rubbed his back. "But to answer your question, Winslet was born and raised in Fallport. Every so often she teaches for a semester at the local university when she's not out on some dig, or doing work for the National History of Crime and Punishment Museum, or being called by the FBI, CIA, or some other agency who needs her brand of expertise."

"Sounds like that character on the hit TV show *Bones.*"

"Exactly. And she's way out of your fucking league." Zeke paused in front of a booth in the back of the restaurant where five men were enjoying a few pitchers of beer. "Boys, this is my buddy Jett. He's our newest park ranger." He pointed to the man in the corner. "That guy is Lincoln. He was Special Boat Service in the UK. Next to him is Brock. He worked Customs Border Patrol. Across the table there is Ethan and Rocky. Both SEALs. But I believe you met them a few years back."

"We did. Nice to see you again." Jett nodded.

"And next to Rocky is his cousin Weston. He's a local cop here in town and a former ranger," Zeke said.

"Damn." Jett smiled. "Long time no see. Weston and I did Ranger School together. I had no idea you landed here." Jett stretched out his arm.

"This is a good town to wind up in. Why don't you have a seat? We were just about to order some appetizers." He glanced at his watch. "I've got two hours before the wife says I've got to be home to help her with getting the little rug rats down for the night."

"Married with kids." Jett slipped into the booth. "Last time our paths crossed you swore commitment wasn't in your future."

"When you meet my Haven, you'll understand why

she changed my mind on that." Weston laughed. "Where's Kiki?"

"Oh, we divorced about six years ago," Jett said.

"I'll go get another pitcher and bring over a platter of appetizers." Zeke tapped his knuckles on the table. "Be nice to my boy here. I'll be back."

"Sorry to hear about you and Kiki." Weston lifted his beer and took a slow slip. "When we went to Ranger School, you'd only been married for a little while."

"Marriage didn't last that long," Jett admitted, glancing over his shoulder.

Winslet and her friends were dropping back a shot and laughing.

"Zeke tells us that you're moving into the apartments in town," Weston said. "I lived there for a while. Not a bad place. Did you get the studio or the one-bedroom?"

"One-bedroom. I already dropped off my stuff a little while ago. Not bad. I honestly expected a dump by the way Zeke described it, but it's nicer than most places I've lived in. And it was furnished, which was helpful."

"My wife, Stormi, and I live around the corner," Lincoln said. "Feel free to reach out if you need anything."

"Any of us at Search and Rescue are more than happy to lend a hand to our park rangers." Brock raised his beer. "It's pretty quiet out there, but we're coming up on our busy season and every year something weird happens."

"Yeah, like when Madison's sister went missing. That was a hard case," Rocky said.

"Who's Madison?" Jett found himself staring at Winslet and not his new friends.

"Brayden's wife. He's a fellow Search and Rescue man. You'll meet him soon enough. Good guy," Ethan said. "Old friend of mine and my brother's."

"We recruit a lot that way." Lincoln chuckled. "Are we checking out Winslet or one of her friends?"

Jett snapped his gaze back to the men sitting at the table and cleared his throat. "None of them."

Everyone laughed.

"Winslet is a real looker, that's for sure," Ethan said. "She's a good woman, too. But unless you're looking for anything other than a fling, I wouldn't chase after that one."

"Are you suggesting she leaves a trail of broken hearts behind?" Jett shouldn't have asked the question. But when a woman was known for something, and that lady had the ability turn his head, he wanted to know what it was that had people talking.

Especially if it was a reason that should keep his wandering eye from wandering to her. Not that he was interested.

Because he wasn't.

He came to Fallport for a job. For a fresh start. That

didn't include getting tangled up with the likes of the female persuasion. At least not right out of the gate.

"She doesn't do relationships," Weston said. "She's here through the end of the semester and maybe through the summer, depending on what her work life tosses her way and how she gets along with her folks. But when she does come to town, she often finds some guy, has a fling, then breaks his heart when she leaves. It's not like she doesn't warn the guy, and the locals all know she's not staying in town for the long haul."

One thing Jett knew about people and relationships was that there was always a reason they didn't do them. He had his, and they were good ones. If Winslet didn't want to be in one for any length of time, something in her past dictated that response.

"She's been here since Christmas and, to our knowledge, hasn't been with anyone." Brock raised his hand. "Not that we sit around and gossip about Winslet."

"But our wives do." Weston laughed. "Haven has known Winslet her entire life and it's kind of pissed her off that Winslet can bounce from one man to the next and not be called a slut. But be treated like a man and everyone just states it's one more notch on her bedpost."

"Yeah, but men in this town treat her like she's a challenge." Rocky arched a brow. "As if they can tame her of her wild ways, which is gross if you ask me.

She's a person, not a prize, and those men aren't good enough for her anyway."

"Besides, she's got family demons," Weston said.

"Maybe that's why she hasn't dated anyone this semester. Or perhaps everyone has finally learned that Winslet is not marriage material and stopped trying," Ethan said.

Jett turned, eyeing the beauty once more. "I've had a failed marriage and if that has taught me anything, it's that not only am I not long-haul relationship material, but that when others make judgments about that fact, it's because they don't understand it. No offense."

"Absolutely none taken, and most of us might say we were once of that philosophy," Weston said. "So, now I'm curious, are you saying you'd hit on her for a fling?"

"If that's the case, we might shut you down." Rocky cocked his head. "You might be a good man, and Winslet is a grown woman, capable of taking care of herself. However, something has been bothering her ever since she's come back to town. We don't know what it is, and she's chosen to keep to herself outside of hanging with her team."

"I'm simply curious since we're talking about it." Jett rubbed his hip. The one that didn't have metal holding it together. The doctors told him he was lucky both didn't need to be replaced.

He wasn't so sure about that.

"I came here to work and that's what I'm going to

do. You boys decided to fill me in on that one. I'm just enjoying the view," he said.

"Well, don't enjoy it too much." Lincoln laughed. "Unless you want to go down that road." He waggled his finger. "Because she's eyeing you too and you're new in this town. She might take you up on that."

"Noted." Jett leaned back as a waitress appeared carrying a tray of food, making his mouth water.

"There's one more thing you should know about Winslet," Rocky said.

"Why? I'm not entertaining any thoughts about her." Jett had numerous thoughts jumping around his brain. But they were thoughts he had no intention of acting on.

"Because as the newest park ranger, you'll hear about her grandfather, who was also a park ranger," Brock said. "He disappeared when her father was fourteen years old, right after her grandmother was found murdered in their kitchen. Shot in the back. Marcus has never been found and the murder is still unsolved."

"I've read the file." Weston pushed his plate aside. "One of the cold cases that sits on my desk and taunts me."

"Weston here hates unsolved crimes," Rocky said.

"With a passion. And that case is a head-scratcher." Weston rubbed the back of his neck. "Lola, Winslet's grandmother, was well-liked in the community. So was Marcus, and according to everyone who knew them, they loved each other dearly. They were high school sweethearts, and her murder rocked this community. No one wanted to believe Marcus could have killed his wife. But all the evidence points to Marcus." Weston lifted his beer. "But then came the rumors. And there are a lot of rumors. Most don't make sense."

"I take it this is her family demon." Jett was more than intrigued by the tale. "What kind of evidence? And are the rumors founded?"

"The murder weapon, a shotgun, was left at the scene. The bullets matched and the only prints on the weapon were that of Marcus. A note was left behind, stating he was sorry. Forensics states that the handwriting is a match for Marcus," Weston said. "But it only says he was sorry. We don't know for what. And there is Hannah Wilks who left her husband the same day of the murder. She left him a note, stating she was in love with Marcus. That they had been having an affair and they were leaving town. She's never been heard from since. That note also passes handwriting forensics, but no one can believe it. Cooper and Hannah loved each other. And the two couples were good friends. Unless they were swingers, it's a big leap." He arched a brow. "Lots of speculation on the possibility that Cooper Wilks killed them all, but Cooper maintains his innocence. He still lives in town, and there is no evidence to support that theory. He never remarried and he's been a broken man ever since. Not just over his wife, but over what he believes are the deaths of his friends. Oddly enough, he believes

Winslet's dad killed his parents. But that's about as fucked up as it comes."

"Are you still actively investigating this?" Jett asked.

"We don't have a cold case department here in Fallport," Weston said. "County and State are too damn busy to give a damn. So yeah, I look into it when I can. So does my wife. But it's about as cold as the artic snow. Why, are you looking to do some moonlighting for the police department?"

"Good grief, no." Jett laughed. "When I'm not at the ranger station, out on the trails, or volunteering for Search and Rescue, I plan on fishing, camping, and taking a few little road trips."

"And maybe taking in the sights?" Brock asked. "Or should I say, taking out a sight named Winslet."

"Zeke warned me that you all were a bunch of ballbusters." Jett laughed before bringing his beer to his lips. The problem was, he was too intrigued by her good looks, her laugh, and the history. But not enough to strike up a conversation.

At least not tonight.

"But if I get bored out there on ranger duty and you want another set of eyes on those files, I would humor you."

## CHAPTER TWO

Winslet wrapped her arms around her best friend. The evening had been a soiree of emotions, both good and bad. But Winslet held the worst of them close to her chest. She plastered a smile on her face and forced herself to have a good time. And it wasn't the worst evening. She enjoyed her friends. The banter. The laughter. The lightness of it all. "Thanks for tonight. I sorely needed it."

"You haven't been yourself lately and I'm sorry that it ended up being about me. I hadn't meant to do that. I wanted to tell you in private, but it was hard because I can't drink, and everyone was pushing me as to the reason why I wasn't partaking." Emory held her by the forearms and gave her that look. It was the slight tilt of her head with a lowered chin.

God, Winslet hated it when anyone pitied her, but it

twisted her guts like a blender when it came from Emory.

"I'm happy for you. I truly am." That was the truth. But Winslet would be lying to herself if she said the news hadn't stung like a bee. A little pinch at first. No big deal. However, seconds later, that sting grew and decayed into a pain that drove a person crazy.

"I know it's been a few months since your breakup with Shamus, and you keep telling me it was bound to happen, but you loved him. And don't try to tell me otherwise."

Being in love had been an unwanted complication in Winslet's life. She'd met Shamus a year ago at a conference. What started out as a wild weekend romance turned into an eight-month love affair that had rocked her world. Everything she thought she wanted her life to be changed in an instant because she loved Shamus so completely.

Until she found out the bastard had been lying to her the entire time.

Winslet had been the female version of a player. She never lasted very long with a guy, but she never lied or led them on. Every man she ever dated knew the score. Winslet Payne wasn't going to get married or have children.

She'd thought about it once when she'd been twenty-two. What a mistake that had been, and she swore she'd never let another man have her heart. Or tell her what to do or how to do it. So, when she hooked up with Shamus, she fought her feelings from the get-go.

But three months in, she couldn't do it anymore.

She loved him with everything she was and was willing to change her stripes.

They talked about marriage and what it might look like for them, including where they might settle. He even asked her if she wanted children.

Or maybe it was she who brought it up first.

It didn't matter.

But now she was left with an unyielding need for something different. It wasn't that she wanted it with Shamus anymore, because she didn't. That was over and she wouldn't go back. Not even if he left his wife.

She shivered at that thought. Winslet was no home-wrecker.

"It's weird to say we broke up when I found out he was married already." Winslet let out a puff of air. Tears no longer stung her eyes, but the shame of it all burned her heart like a cattle prod. She was a smart woman. The fact she hadn't seen the signs still tore through her soul like an out-of-control beast racing through the wilderness. When she'd learned the truth, she immediately withdrew her request for a guest lecture at the same college he'd accepted a position. Did he not think she'd find out when she got to town? She wanted them to live together. How would that have been possible when he brought his wife and two kids?

Fucker.

"He's an asshole and I'm glad you found out before you did something even crazier. Like accepted a full-time professorship." Emory smiled that sweet grin of hers that made Winslet melt. "Though, you know, I'll follow you almost anywhere. I love being your assistant both in the teaching world and in the forensics lab."

"What about being my best friend?"

Emory laughed. "That one goes without saying." She kissed her cheek. "Are you sure you're going to be okay? I'm worried that you are going to respond to his message."

"I'm not going to give him the satisfaction. One more drink, and then I'm going to walk home. I'll see you on Monday. Enjoy the weekend with Oscar. He's a good egg and I'm so excited for both of you. I really am."

"He's going to be totally shocked, even though we've been trying for a year now." Emory turned on her heel and strolled out the front door.

Winslet sighed. She wasn't jealous of Emory and her husband. Far from it. She loved Oscar like a brother. His job as a data project manager for one of the largest marketing firms in North America made it so he could work from anywhere. It did require some travel. Lots of conference calls. But they didn't come any better than Oscar. He adored Emory and treated her like a princess.

Glancing at the bar, she groaned. Only one seat open, right next to the sexy newcomer. She'd heard all about Zeke's buddy, the great Jett McCoy. The man who nearly died a little over a year ago. A true hero. For the past few weeks, Zeke had been bristling with excitement over Jett's arrival. It was all that man could talk about.

Oh, how this town would gossip if she plopped herself down next to him.

But if she wanted a nightcap in a room full of people so she didn't feel like she was drinking alone, she didn't have a choice. There wasn't an open table left and now that Emory was going to be gone for the weekend, Winslet wanted to get shitfaced here because it was the only way Winslet would get through the night without calling Shamus.

Sad, but true.

And if she did end up speaking with Shamus, the next call would be to Emory, and she would have something to say about that.

Not that Emory would be too harsh over it all, but still. There would be words. Emory would start in on how there were other fish in the sea because at the end of the day, Shamus wasn't going to leave his wife, and Winslet didn't want him to. At least not for her. She wasn't that girl.

And Winslet didn't want another fish. She didn't want Shamus either. All she wanted was to get lost in her work, but so far, no new dig had come her way, and no weird bones had been unearthed either.

Besides, she had to reconcile the fact that if she

took an assignment in some foreign country, the likelihood that Emory would follow now that she was pregnant was slim to none.

Winslet would have to find another assistant if she made that choice, a reality she had to accept.

She hoisted herself up on the bench. "Hey, Zeke, can I get a straight tequila with a lime."

"Coming up." Zeke wiped down the counter. "Have you met my buddy Jett?" he asked with a wide smile.

"Can't say that I have, and I'm shocked you're making the introductions." She took the glass Zeke offered and raised it.

"I warned him about you." Zeke chuckled, waggling his index finger. "In a kind and loving sort of way."

"Of course you did." She'd known Zeke for as long as he'd owned this bar, and that was too many years to count. He was like that weird older cousin who was always there, watching over her, waiting to catch her when she fell.

And he had once or twice.

Zeke had a big heart, and he loved hard. She was lucky to call him friend. If anyone else had made that kind of comment, she wouldn't have taken it in the sarcastic way that Zeke had delivered it.

Jett coughed and pounded the center of his chest. "You should be offended." He raised his drink. "I'm offended for you."

She shrugged. "Nah. It would be like me not telling one of my girlfriends about that guy over there." She jerked her thumb over her shoulder. "Talk about a player. Only, he comes on like he's all madly in love with you. Treats you all special, and then next thing you know, he's banging someone else. All Zeke here did was probably tell you I'm a straight shooter who never stays in one place too long and I haven't had a real boyfriend since I was in my early twenties." She tilted her head back and downed her drink as if it were a tall glass of ice water. "Only, that's not entirely true since the whole reason no one in this town can gossip about my bed partners this semester is because I let some asshole into my heart, and he ripped it from my chest." She waved her glass under Zeke's nose. "Fill her up and leave the bottle." Resenting the idea her best friend was about to start a family made her want to crawl under the bar because she really wasn't upset over Emory's good news. It wasn't that at all. It was merely the fact she'd wanted that too.

With a married man.

How awful was that?

"Jesus, Winslet. What happened?" Zeke poured a single shot in her glass. Jerk. She'd wanted a double. Or maybe a triple. "Does this man need me to teach him a lesson? Because you know I will."

"That's real sweet of you." She sucked in a deep breath. The fact that Emory was going to tell Oscar he was about to become a father this weekend had brought all these emotions back to the surface, and adding that Shamus had reached out, asking if they could talk, shouldn't be the reason she told Zeke or a perfect stranger. But what were good bartenders for? "Since his wife still doesn't know about me, nor do his kids, and I don't want to be a homewrecker, it's best you keep your fists to yourself."

Zeke set the bottle on the counter with a thud. "Don't get pissed, but did you know?"

"That's a fair question and the answer is absolutely not," she said. "I found out when I showed up early to the same place we were scheduled to give a lecture. He was kissing her and his kids goodbye. Talk about a shock."

"That sucks for both you, her, and the kids." Jett reached across the bar, lifted the bottle of tequila, and refilled his glass. "But if you didn't know, you're not the homewrecker, he is, and if you were in her shoes, wouldn't you want to know?"

"The moral dilemma of the last few months of my life." She clanked her glass against his before downing her drink in one gulp. The effects of the alcohol she'd consumed that evening hit her brain like a rocket ship hurling through the atmosphere. "However, I'm still not going to be the one to tell her. I already feel like a skank. That would make me feel like a whore."

Zeke took her hand. "I don't want to ever hear that word come out of your mouth. You might be a little rough around the edges, but a whore, you are not."

"Thanks, Zeke, but I have to ask. If you don't think

that way about me, why do you and all your buddies warn men about me?"

"For the record, I've never said a bad thing. But I think you know that. And it's not a warning." Zeke lowered his chin and took her hand. "After what happened with Harvey, we all believed you'd never go down that road again."

"Who's Harvey?" Jett asked.

"My ex-fiancé." She shivered. "Three days before I was set to marry that asshole, I found him in bed with the chick I hired to do the alterations to my wedding dress. That bitch never did give me my money back." She poured more tequila into her glass, ignoring Zeke and his friend, who stared at her with wide, judgmental eyes. Or at least she believed they judged her. Hell, she often judged herself, but only because the events of her past still held her present—and future—hostage. "No. I'm not bitter. Not really. I mean, they are standing the test of time." She shrugged. "And I heard she's pregnant with their third. Who am I to stand in the way of true love? But let's just say that after spending years swearing I'd never do it again, well, it just sucks that I had to fall for a dick."

"You and Jett seem to have that in common." Zeke took the bottle and put it behind the bar.

She turned. "Really? You have shit taste in boyfriends?" She hiccupped.

Jett chuckled. "You're funny. And also very drunk.

Give me your keys so I can make sure you get home safely."

"I walked." She hiccupped again. Not a good sign.

"Well, then I will walk you home," Jett said.

"She's subleasing in your building." Zeke glanced at his watch. "I need to get home. Told the wife I was just coming in to hang for a few hours with the guys and do some paperwork. I'll see you two later. Those last few drinks were on the house." He pressed his hand on the counter. "Winslet, call me if you need anything. I know I give you a fair amount of shit, but we've known each other a long time. I've got your back. Anything you need, even if all you want is to talk."

"I know you do, and I need to reach out to Weston and Haven and thank them for always keeping my grandparents' case on their desk. I know they don't have to do that." She covered her mouth as another belch flew from her lips.

"Make sure she gets home okay." Zeke waved his finger. "Call me in the morning."

"Will do." Jett nodded.

Damn man was a fucking Boy Scout.

If she wasn't well on her way to being falling down wasted, she'd tell Zeke to take a hike, along with his incredibly sexy friend. But considering all the tequila she consumed, she'd be passed out in less than an hour. She grabbed Mr. Tall-Drink-of-Something's arm and squeezed. Wow, that was an impressive biceps. "Come on. I need to get home. Sorry if that was before you wanted to leave, but I'm beyond my limit and I know more than one idiot in this bar who might be willing to take advantage of a drunk girl."

He helped her from the stool and guided her through the sea of staring people. The gossip mills would be all abuzz in the morning. Wonderful.

"And how are you so sure I wouldn't?" He cocked a brow.

"Because you're friends with Zeke." She stumbled through the front door. "His buddies aren't like that and if they were, he'd kick the shit out of them." She looped her arm through his, giving it a good hug. "Don't care how muscular you are." She glanced up. "Or that you have to be close to six foot four, he'd hurt you."

"I'm six three and he'd put me six feet under." He looped his arm around her waist. "My truck's right over there."

"I'd rather walk. It will be fine there for the night."

"Whatever you say." He nodded. "Mind if I ask you a personal question?"

"Shoot."

"Why do you let people talk about you like that?"

She let out a long breath. "First, other people's opinions of me aren't my business. Second, I can't control what the world thinks of me. And third, it used to work in keeping any man who wanted anything other than a good time far away. Now all I get are those trying to tame me. Make an honest woman out of me.

Well, after what Shamus did, I think I'll sleep in the middle of the bed for a while."

Jett laughed. "Not all men are assholes, just like I'm sure not all women are heartless bitches."

"Sounds like someone's speaking from experience." She paused, bent over, and kicked out of her heels. She rarely wore the suckers but thought it might be nice to dress herself up today. Stupid idea.

"Are you sure you want to go barefoot? We still have three more blocks to go."

"I'll be fine," she said. "Now, since I most likely won't remember half this conversation, why don't you tell me about why you're harboring some resentment against my sex."

"That's not exactly what I'm doing." They paused at the red light two streets over from the apartment building. "My ex-wife divorced me because I was cold. Unfeeling. Emotionally unavailable. According to her, and I'm not going to deny it, I was more interested in my career and my buddies than I was her."

"Then why did you get married?"

"I didn't say I didn't love her, because as much as I'm capable of loving someone who isn't blood, or who isn't going into battle with me, she rocked my world. But for her, it was a one-sided relationship and one day, I came home, and it was just over. I knew she was unhappy. We fought all the time. But what I didn't know was that she'd already checked out and was seeing someone else."

"How did that make you feel?"

"I was angry for like five seconds. Truth is, I didn't love her enough to fight for her, but I loved her enough to let her go."

"I think that's the most mature thing I've ever heard a man say." She leaned into his strong body, resting her head on his shoulder as they strolled toward the next crosswalk. "Any other big romances?"

"Not sure I'd call it big, but right before I nearly died in a helicopter crash about sixteen months ago, I was seeing this girl. She couldn't deal with my injuries. Six months after the accident, she bailed."

Winslet glanced up, catching his gaze. She liked the timbre of his voice and enjoyed how he had no problem sharing his broken heart stories. But he did so in a flat, unfeeling manner that unsettled her insides. "How bad was it, outside of the near-death experience? I mean, all Zeke said was you were mortally wounded."

He chuckled. "Let's just say I'm lucky I can walk, and I have more metal in me than a half dozen senior citizens combined."

"Ouch. That sounds painful."

"It was."

She hiccupped. Not once. Not twice. But three times in a row. "Sorry."

"No worries." He paused at the base of their building.

"I have a feeling that I might end up spending half

the night in front of the toilet. And tomorrow's going to suck in a different way."

"Probably." He unlocked the door. "What floor and what apartment?"

"I'm in 1B. I sublet it from this guy who finished up his master's degree last year and was waiting to hear about a job. It came through right before Christmas, which was nice because I really didn't want to live with my parents."

"Looks like we're neighbors, since I just signed a year lease for 1A."

Her stomach sloshed and swished like a dead fish on a roller-coaster ride. This was so not a good idea. She lifted her finger and punched in her passcode but fumbled it the first try. "Shit," she mumbled. Leaning forward, squinting, she tried again.

The little thing beeped, and the lock twisted. She flung the door open and tripped over… she had no idea what.

"I got you." Jett circled his arms around her body.

Her hands came down on his solid chest. She blinked, staring up into his dark orbs. "Thsank you for making sssure I got hom swaftly." Her tongue felt like it stuck to the roof of her mouth.

"Anytime." He brushed her hair from her face. "I don't feel right about leaving you here alone."

"I'll be fine." While she appreciated Jett walking her home, simply because she most likely wouldn't have made it by herself, all she wanted to do now was shed her clothes and empty her stomach.

And she didn't want to do that with him around.

"You had enough booze to choke a horse. Someone needs to watch over you."

"Not neces... Oh God." She pushed from his embrace and raced off toward the bathroom. While she could normally handle her liquor, the double shots after a few glasses of wine and some shots in between to celebrate Emory's good news—well, that was a lot, even for her.

She dropped to her knees, lifted the seat, and let her stomach revolt.

And revolt.

God, she hated being sick. At least this part wouldn't last. Or so she hoped. She wiped her lips, flushed, and rested her head on the toilet, letting out a long breath. Maybe she should sleep right here.

Yeah. That was a solid plan.

Why did she think returning to this town would be a good idea? All it did was remind her that her family was always the center of the town gossip, thanks to her grandfather—and father. Which was only made worse because she'd been basically left standing at the altar.

"Here. Drink this."

She jerked, stiffening her spine, remembering she'd left Jett in the other room. She glanced over her shoulder and groaned. "How long have you been standing there holding that bottle of water?"

"Does it really matter?" He bent over, looped his arm around her waist, and guided her into the only other room. Gently, he laid her on the bed, shoving the water in her face and a bucket next to her pillow. "Seriously, you need to hydrate." He pointed toward the dresser. "What drawer are your pajamas in?"

She dribbled water all down her chin. "Excuse me?"

He didn't bother glancing over his shoulder. Instead, he yanked open the top one and pulled out a pair of boxers and a tank top.

"Yeah. That will do." She shimmied out of her jeans and yanked up the boxers he tossed in her direction. "Turn around."

"No problem," he said with a chuckle.

After she finished changing her top, she crawled between the sheets and closed her eyes, thankful the room didn't spin.

But the bed did shift. And rock. And squeak.

She sighed.

"Thanks for seeing me home. The door will lock thirty seconds after you leave."

"Just close your eyes and rest," Jett whispered.

She hugged her pillow and prayed that she'd sleep right through the weekend and most likely the worst hangover known to man.

# CHAPTER THREE

Jett sat at the small kitchen table, palming a mug of coffee and staring at sleeping beauty who certainly knew how to snore. Then again, if he'd packed away as much tequila as she had, he probably would have sounded like a grizzly, too.

At least she hadn't gotten sick in her sleep. That had been his biggest fear, and he would wake nearly every thirty minutes to check on her. He always found it comical that both Kiki and Becky had referred to him as inattentive. Uncaring. Cold even. He knew he could come off as dry. He definitely had an odd sense of humor.

But he did care.

It was showing it in the ways they demanded that had been the hard part.

He swiped at the screen on his iPad, shocked she hadn't woken when he'd left to get the gadget. While there were plenty of reading materials, he wanted to learn more about her family history, specifically her grandparents, but more importantly, he wanted to google her.

Perhaps that made him a creeper. Stalker. Or an all-around jerk.

His ex-wife thought he never cared enough about her thoughts or feelings. That he took her for granted. She would never accuse him of not being a gentleman in the sense that he always opened doors for her, remembered their anniversary, and brought her flowers. And when they were dating, he paid for everything.

But Kiki had told him after a few months of living together, that his grand gesture of remembering to put the toilet seat down regularly meant shit when he couldn't be bothered to ask her about her day and actually listen as if he cared. The thing was, he did care. He just didn't care about the color of her nails. Or if she should cut her hair shorter or let it grow. And the one time he did comment, she'd been so pissed, she told him to sleep on the sofa.

Of course, a friend mentioned, after the fact, that telling his wife he liked her hair better longer, after she'd chopped it off, wasn't winning any brownie points. The time for bringing that up might have been when she asked for his opinion three weeks before.

But it was her hair. His opinion shouldn't matter. However, because of all the fights over these stupid little things, he thought maybe he should be honest.

That hadn't worked. He couldn't win.

He focused his attention on the article Winslet had written regarding some case she'd solved for the FBI. Impressive, though he didn't understand half of it. He had to look up at least ten words already that she'd used in the article regarding forensics and anthropology, and he still didn't really get it.

The girl was mad wicked smart.

Made him feel like a dope. He could stitch up a guy with his guts hanging out in the field. He knew more about human anatomy than the average person. But he didn't know dick compared to Winslet.

A groan echoed through the tiny studio apartment. He glanced over the iPad and watched Winslet stretch and roll.

She had to be the prettiest girl he'd ever laid eyes on, even with her hair in a tangled mess and last night's makeup smudged on her face.

He chuckled.

"What the hell?" She clutched the sheets, bolted to an upright position, and moaned like a dying cow.

That shouldn't be sexy, but damn if it was.

"I wouldn't move that quickly if I were you," he said.

"Why are you here?" She brushed her hair from her face and rubbed her temples. "I should call the police."

"But you won't." He swiped at the screen of his tablet, closing out the browser, and stood. "Would you like some coffee?" He lifted his empty mug. "And maybe some greasy hangover food?"

"Yes, and yes," she said. "Did you sleep here?"

He nodded.

"Where?" she asked with wide eyes.

"On the sofa." He pointed to the tiny couch next to the fireplace. For a studio, it wasn't horrible. It had to be about five hundred square feet. Enough for a bed, a couple pieces of furniture for a makeshift living room. The kitchen was small but had enough space for a table and two chairs.

"Well, aren't you the gentleman," she mumbled. "But not really. You should have left me to sleep it off alone."

"I couldn't do that. Not after watching you make love to the porcelain god." He stuffed a pod in the coffee maker and pressed the button after placing a large mug in the proper spot. He leaned against the counter and folded his arms across his chest. "I was honestly worried you might get sick in your sleep."

"I wasn't that bad." She swung her legs to the side and gripped the mattress. "Okay, so maybe I was." She leaned back on the pillows, covering her eyes with her forearm. "But now you can leave me to suffer my embarrassment alone."

"After I feed you. Now, what would you like? You have the fixings for eggs or maybe French Toast."

"There's a breakfast sandwich maker in the cupboard. But I can manage my own food."

"Yeah. Right. I don't think you'll be doing much of anything today but lying in that bed and binge-watching television." He found the appliance she described. He'd seen one of these things before. He and Kiki had gotten one as a wedding present, though he'd never actually used it himself. It couldn't be that hard. Kiki had made him more than one sandwich in it. She would send him off to the base with one wrapped in foil. She was good about things like that. Too good. Sometimes it was stifling. To him, marriage was a partnership. With Kiki, it felt like he'd been transported back to the fifties. He pulled out all the ingredients necessary and plugged in the machine.

"Since I don't have the strength to argue with you and I really want that food, would you mind handing me my purse? I need to check my messages and charge my cell."

"Sure." Once he had everything he needed in the little sandwich machine, he set his timer, then strolled across the room, snagged her purse, and set it gently on the bed. "Zeke texted me this morning asking how you were."

"I hope you didn't tell him you spent the night here."

"He'd be pissed if I had left you alone, so of course I did."

"Fucking wonderful." She dug into her purse, tapped her screen, and groaned. "It's dead." She leaned to the side and set it on her charger.

"Probably a good thing. You mumbled a few times as you were falling asleep about how you needed to stay away from your phone. Something about not texting or calling that prick."

"I don't think I want to know what I might have told you last night."

"Not that much, but enough." His timer went off. He made his way back to the kitchen, pulled out a plate, and flipped the sandwich on it. Damn, that was easy. He was going to have to get himself one of these things. It would save him a lot of money. Quickly, he made a second one before bringing her the food and her coffee. "Now that you're sober, let me say, I'm real sorry about what that jerk did." He handed her a mug and set the plate on the bed. Easing onto the couch across from her, he sipped his own coffee and nibbled on his sandwich, trying not to allow his physical attraction for a woman he barely knew to cloud his good judgment.

But it wasn't going to be easy.

It had been a long time since he'd even thought about being with a lady. Before the crash, he had a girlfriend, and he liked her a whole lot. More than most. So much, he found himself thinking crazy thoughts. So, when she freaked out, he couldn't deny it hurt. But he didn't put up much of a fight. She'd dumped him while he was at his worst, and he had a bigger war to deal with.

Another surgery. More rehab. More physical and emotional battles. He couldn't cope with the pain of losing a girl who struggled with his chosen career path anyway.

Since then, his life had been all about gaining his

physical strength back and figuring out what to do next. The Army and Special Forces were no longer an option. Not unless he wanted a desk job, and he decided it was time to try his hand at something else.

Women were not on his radar. Not even for a one-night stand. So, he hadn't even entertained the idea.

Only, if Winslet hadn't been so wasted last night, he would have thought about it. Hell, he was thinking about it now.

"I'm partially to blame for what happened with Shamus." Winslet brought the mug to her mouth and blew before taking a slow sip. The way her lips curled over the rim was intoxicating.

What the fuck was his problem?

Perhaps it was going nearly eighteen months without sex.

Or maybe it was watching her sleep for hours.

Jesus, he was an asshole.

"If you didn't know he was married, I don't see how," he said. "When my ex-wife informed me she had been having an affair, my initial reaction was to go find that man and beat the shit out of him. Who did he think he was to sleep with another man's wife?" He waggled his finger. "But the thing is, he didn't know at first because Kiki didn't tell him. It wasn't until she left me that she clued him in."

"Are they still together?"

"No," Jett said. "I don't know if they broke up because she lied to him about being married or if there were other factors. And it's not my business. She and I weren't going to stay married regardless. She was miserable and I was a shit husband. I can admit that. But my point is, I can't blame him for something he didn't know."

"Maybe. However, I should have seen the signs. They were right there in front of me. The secrecy. The backpedaling when I started committing to the relationship." She set her mug on the nightstand. "I have to wonder if he chose me because I didn't want to get married or have children."

Jett arched a brow. "I take it that changed."

Her cell dinged as it powered on. She glanced toward it and audibly groaned. "I really don't want to talk about this."

"I've got no skin in this game." He polished off the rest of his breakfast, stood, and eased onto the bed, fluffing the pillow.

She glared.

"We don't know each other. We have no history, and believe me, I'm not judging. Of all the women I've dated in my life, I can only say I've had two real relationships and both of them, I was a dick in different ways. Both were doomed more because of me first, then them."

"Are you trying to tell me you understand Shamus? Because I can't for the life of me figure him out." She pointed to her cell. "Or why after months of not hearing from him, he's all of a sudden texting and calling, telling me we need to talk. He's relentless."

"No. I can't comprehend what he did. I've never cheated on anyone. I'm not that guy." He tapped her knee. "I have broken up with women because I became interested in someone else, so that makes me an asshole."

"An honest asshole." She laughed. "Can I ask you a question?"

"Sure."

"The girl who dumped you after the crash, what was her problem? I mean, that's a shit thing to do. It feels like she kicked you when you were down."

He glanced toward the ceiling. He wasn't bitter over Becky dumping him, and on some level, he understood her reason and certainly her emotions behind it. "Becky already struggled with my military career. Not everyone is cut out to be involved with someone in the Army. But I was Special Forces. I was often deployed more than I was Stateside. I couldn't talk about my missions. It wasn't like we could go out to dinner when I returned home and chat about the things that I did. But that crash was personal for her."

"I would say so. Her boyfriend nearly died."

"It was more than that. Her brother was a news correspondent in the area. He was covering a story. I didn't know he was on the ground. I also didn't know that he was one of the people we were going in to evacuate and rescue. He died that day, and she ended up blaming me for his death." He leaned over and pressed his finger over Winslet's plump lips. He was going to have to do something to squelch his attraction. It wasn't good for either of them. "At first, she didn't. Or at least she tried not to. Especially when the doctors told me that it was possible I might not ever walk again. But as I improved and made great progress, she started resenting me. After I was officially awarded a medal for saving two lives that day, she lost her shit because I couldn't save her brother. Thing was, the helicopter went down miles before that extraction point. He was dead before we even got close. I know I'm not responsible. But she'll always blame me and the two other survivors. There isn't anything I can do about that."

"Anyone ever tell you that you're too accepting of things?"

He chuckled. "More like selfish. I was facing more surgeries. It was still a major uphill battle. I didn't have it in me to fight for her. For us. What does that say about how I really felt about her?"

"Where is she now?"

"Back home. But I haven't kept tabs on her. I focused on my recovery. I haven't spoken to her in months." He waggled his finger. "You're very good at changing the subject."

"I have been told that a time or two."

"Your turn." He tucked a few stray strands of her

silky hair behind her ears. "Why are you taking responsibility for Shamus' poor decisions?"

"I'm not. At least not him cheating on his wife. When we first got together, it was at a conference. Then we started applying for the same guest lectures." She dropped her gaze to her lap. "I got offered a dig in Africa, but I needed more than my own team. I told him about it, and he jumped on it. That's when things changed. We were away for three months. We talked about what a future together could look like. We made fucking plans. But when we got back to the States, he started making excuses. His mom was sick. Or his brother was going through stuff. I was working a case with the FBI out in Seattle, and he was teaching in Colorado, but it wasn't a full-time gig, and he told me he wanted to stop running around. To settle down somewhere and he applied for a professorship." She pinched the bridge of her nose. "I keep telling myself that he's the one who told me about the guest lecture spot, but in reality, I'm the one who found it. He didn't tell me not to do it, but he did tell me he was worried that I wasn't the kind of person who would be happy only teaching. He didn't want me there. A couple of times he pushed digs he'd heard about in my face, but always with the idea that he'd support me. God, I was such a fool."

Jett tilted her chin with his thumb and gazed into her eyes. What he saw was less hurt and more shame. "No. Unfortunately, love is blind." He let out a long sigh. "I always say that I didn't fight for Kiki because I didn't love her enough. Or that I loved my career more. The latter might be partially true. If she had ever asked me to give that up—to choose between her and the Army—I'm pretty sure I would have chosen my dog tags. But the reality of that relationship is I was blind to her needs. I thought because I loved her, I didn't need to do anything other than be present. I thought remembering her birthday and doing dorky things on Valentine's Day was enough. But I never saw her for who she was, and I certainly didn't listen."

"I find that hard to believe. You're pretty darn good at it."

"Let me rephrase." He ran his thumb across her cheek, removing some of the mascara that had dribbled across her skin during the night. "I can listen all day long. But I never did anything with the information she gave me. For example, when Kiki explained how lonely she was in our marriage, I got her a puppy to keep her company when I was gone. I thought that would solve that problem. I can see now how she wasn't talking about the time and space when I was deployed but the moments we were in the same house. Hindsight is perfect vision. And while I learned about myself because of those failed relationships, I also learned I'm still a selfish bastard who isn't going to change, nor do I want to." He dropped his hand to his lap. "But we're back to me again." He pointed to her phone, which was currently vibrating, and Shamus' name had appeared on the screen. "Would you like me to answer that? It might help to send the message that you don't want to talk."

She reached for her cell and tossed it to him. "Sure. Drive the point home. But put it on speaker. I want to hear this."

"Hello?" He cleared his throat.

"Who is this?" a male voice asked with an indignant tone. "Where's Winslet?"

"She's unavailable at the moment," Jett said. "Actually, she's unavailable to you forever. So, please stop calling and texting her."

"Yeah, I'm going to need her to tell me that. So, please, put Winslet on the phone," Shamus said.

"Sorry. She doesn't want to speak to you. I'm going to hang—"

"And you are?"

"Jett. The boyfriend." He winked.

She rolled her eyes, shaking her head.

At least she didn't slap him.

"Right. Maybe a rebound one-night stand," Shamus said. "Tell Winslet to call me. It's important. And time sensitive. Tell her I need to hear from her in the next couple of days." The line went dead.

"When hell freezes over will I ever communicate with that man again." She hopped to her feet. "Oh God. I did that too fast." She leaned over, pressing her hands on the bed. "It's going to be a long day."

"Lucky for you, I have no plans but to binge-watch mindless television with you."

She stood tall and narrowed her stare. "You're not my boyfriend and we are not going to lounge around on a lazy Saturday together. Thanks for being a nice guy. But there's the door."

"Who's going to help you stay strong when Shamus calls back? Because we both know he's going to. He called three times yesterday and I saw a string of texts."

"Anyone ever tell you that you're a nosy fuck?" She picked up her pillow and tossed it at his face.

He chuckled. "I can't say that happens too often." He raised his hands. "I'll leave. But on one condition."

"I'm terrified to hear what this is."

"You let me cook you dinner tonight. I'll go buy some nice steaks and we can grill them up and enjoy a good bottle of wine."

She rubbed her temples. "Not sure my body will be ready for alcohol, but a girl has to eat." She padded around the bed and stretched out her arm. "Now, if you don't mind, I'm going to take a nice long bath, read a book, and go back to sleep for a few hours."

"Oh, that sounds fun. I should join you." He waggled his brows. Shit. This girl had him running in circles.

"Not." She patted his chest. "Thanks for everything. I really do appreciate your kindness."

"Don't mention it." He leaned in and kissed her cheek. "I wrote my number on a piece of paper and left it in the kitchen. Call me if you need anything." He stepped into the hallway and took the ten paces to his front door. He tapped the code on the pad and glanced over his shoulder.

Her door was already shut.

His phone vibrated in his back pocket.

A text from an unknown number that read: *So you have mine, Winslet.*

He smiled, then quickly frowned. Winslet was exactly the kind of woman he enjoyed. She was strong. Intelligent. Funny as hell. And she was genuinely honest. A breath of fresh air.

Exactly the kind of woman he needed to stay away from.

But something told him he wasn't going to be able to do that.

# CHAPTER FOUR

Winslet sat at her kitchen table and stared at her cell. Twenty-five fucking text messages in the last week. Six voice messages. All saying the same thing.

We need to talk.

It's important.

Call me.

But he never once said he was sorry that he hurt her or that he was married. Or that he lied.

She sighed.

What could be so damn important except to apologize for being a dick? Which she'd take in a text message.

When she'd seen him standing outside that hotel, kissing his wife and his two kids, she'd been mortified. Frozen in space and time. Unable to move or say anything. She stood there like a fucking idiot. When he finally saw her, he didn't bat an eyelash. He didn't wave. He didn't even acknowledge she was there. He got in his car service and left.

Didn't even have the decency to call.

Nope. They didn't speak for four days.

She turned around, called an Uber, flew back to Seattle, and informed the department head that she would be unable to give the lecture, hooking them up with someone else. She didn't know what else to do. She'd been heartbroken.

And humiliated.

All in one split second.

When he finally did call, he didn't bother with excuses. Or lies. Or an apology. All he had to say was that things had gotten out of hand, but that he was glad the truth had come out. He was tired of the secrecy. But he also needed to end things. He loved his wife, and he had two kids to think about. He even had the nerve to tell her their names and ages.

As if that would make it easier for *her.*

Well, it only made it worse because it made what she'd done real.

She'd openly had an affair with a married man. She wanted to scrub her body with a Brillo pad.

It would be so easy to call Jett and have him come sit with her while she made this phone call. He was a kind and caring soul. Whatever hang-ups he had in relationships, they didn't spill over in friendships.

But she had to do this on her own. She helped create this mess and she had to put on her big girl panties and deal with it like the grown-up she was.

She tapped Shamus' contact information. It rang twice.

"Finally," Shamus said.

"I take it you're alone." Every word that tumbled out of her mouth dripped with sarcasm and disdain.

"I wouldn't have picked up if I wasn't."

"Of course not. If you had, you might risk someone finding out what a two-timing—"

"I get you're pissed."

"You have no idea what I am, but I'm not angry for me. Not anymore," she said. "However, I didn't call you back to argue with you. Now, what do you want?"

"I just learned that you're teaching this semester in Virginia. After Seattle, I heard you were looking for a dig. Imagine my surprise when I found out you'd taken a position there."

"I've taught here before, and you know that."

"Not the point. I just figured after everything, you'd want to go follow your passion and that's having your hands in the dirt with old bones."

Wow. He didn't really know her at all. While it was true she loved doing that, she much preferred to solve crimes. Working for the FBI, CIA, or any other government agency that wanted to hire out her services, was her true calling. It's one of the many reasons her grandparents' case going unsolved for so long made her nuts. "Why does it matter to you what I do?" she asked.

"Because you had to have known I was on the schedule to give a guest lecture in a couple of weeks."

She dropped her head to the table. So far, two other professors had come in and spoken to different sections of the forensic science department, and she knew there were more scheduled. As a matter of fact, that was always the case. And his coming wouldn't necessarily affect her three courses. While their specialties almost always intersected in the field, he preferred teaching over digging and working criminal cases.

"I haven't seen the list of professors and frankly, I'm not sure how you potentially coming here affects me. We don't have to see each other. Or talk to each other. And if you're scheduled for my courses, I don't even have to introduce you."

"Your team is there. Emory, Jackson, Elizabeth, and Jonah. It would be awkward if you didn't, especially since they all knew about us. And that's what concerns me. I'm bringing my family. It was a planned trip from a few months ago."

She jerked to an upright position, pinched the bridge of her nose, and laughed. Hard. It wasn't funny. Not even close. "To Fallport, Virginia? Where your ex-mistress was born and raised. Why the fuck would you do that? You have got to be as dumb as a doornail."

"I'm not going to get into all the details as to why

this is happening. It's not your business. But I'm sure your team all knows by now that I'm married. I need your assurance that if they run into me and my family, they aren't going to say anything."

"Are you serious right now?" She glared at the phone. What little love she had left for this man flew out the window. "This is what was so fucking important that you had to call me a million times? You're worried your wife is going to find out you're a liar and a cheat? All you want is for me and my friends to help you cover it up after you... you..." No. She wouldn't give him the satisfaction of knowing he'd broken her heart. "Jesus, you're a piece of work."

"I don't think it's too much to ask of you or your friends. My wife hasn't done anything to you. My children are innocent in all this. What do you want me to say?"

"How about I'm sorry for being an asshole," she muttered. "But at this point, it's honestly too late." And sadly, the tears she'd thought she'd already shed and would never come again, flowed down her cheeks like a damn river. They weren't because she loved Shamus. Or even because he'd made a fool of her.

No. They were because her world was different. Thanks to Shamus, she wanted more from life. She wanted a partner, not men she had flings with. She wanted someone to share her life with. Someone she could have a family with.

Maybe she'd wanted that all along and it took

falling in love for her to find that out, but why did she have to fall in love with him?

She hated crying.

It was worse than a fucking hangover.

Or being sloppy drunk and barfing in front of a sexy stranger.

"You have nothing to fear. I'm not a vindictive bitch and my friends would never. If we see you and your family, we'll be professionals. All she'll know is that we've worked together in the past. I wouldn't dream of telling her that your ugly dick was ever in my precious vagina."

"Winslet—"

"Take care, Shamus." She tapped the red button and ended the call. Swiping at her cheeks, she glanced around the studio. It was five in the afternoon. She wasn't due at Jett's for another hour.

Fuck it.

She'd already made an ass out of herself in front of him, what was a cryfest among strangers.

"Evelynn, you'd love it here." Jett adored his little sister. They were only two years apart and best friends. She'd always been his rock. His sounding board. He could tell her anything and everything.

And he did.

Kiki hated it. Resented their relationship. Thought it was weird. Told Jett that if Evelynn had been his brother, she might understand it.

But Evelynn was Jett's only sibling and family was everything to Jett.

"You have to come and visit," he said.

"Oh, I plan on it. But it won't be until July."

"Why so late?" Jett leaned against the mantel and stared out the window. His family room was the size of Winslet's bedroom and living room combined. But his kitchen wasn't much bigger. However, he didn't need much. He was a simple man and living alone made his life much easier.

Although, he did miss some of the fancier things that came with marriage and a partner. But he didn't miss all the damn throw pillows. He would never understand a woman's need for so many pillows.

Including his sister. She might even be worse than any other woman he knew.

"School doesn't get out until the end of June up here. You know that. But both me and Doug will have the entire summer off."

"Ah, the perks of being a teacher and principal." Jett laughed. "Well, I only have one bedroom. It was all I could find on short notice. But maybe we could find something to rent when you and the kids come down. Something with a pool."

"We thought we might want to drive to Georgia to

see his folks. So maybe we could stay with you for five or six days on the way down. See Doug's parents for a week and then stop for a night or two on the way back, but we're talking about leaving the kids with his folks for a couple more weeks, and then they'd fly home later."

"That will work. You know you're welcome anytime. But we need to coordinate with Mom and Dad. I want to buy them airline tickets. But Mom gets so pissy and insists on paying me back. I hate it when she does that."

"Sometimes I swear she forgets you're forty-one and I'm thirty-nine with two kids."

Jett laughed. His parents understood his and Evelynn's bond. The only time things got weird for them was when one of them dated the other's friends.

And that did happen a few times.

They tried not to, but they were close in age and glued together at the hip. They had similar interests and enjoyed the same sports. About the only thing his sister didn't like doing was fishing, but she went with him and his buddies anyway, but more because she wanted to work on her tan.

Doug had been Jett's best friend in high school. Still was a dear friend, but now he was Jett's brother-in-law, and he loved him as though he were blood.

Not to mention their two little crazy monsters.

"Speaking of Mom, when was the last time you spoke with her?" Evelynn asked.

"Right before I called you." Jett rubbed his unshaven face. For years he'd thought about growing a beard, but the military wouldn't let him. Now he thought he just might. "She's still not happy I moved or took this job. She's worried I'm going to fall and snap the metal in my body. I keep trying to tell her this is no different from Grandma's metal hip, but she manages to spew all these reasons why she believes what happened to me is different."

"For Pete's sake, Jett. It's totally different. You're her little boy. And she doesn't narrow it down to your knees and hip. Or even your shoulder surgeries. She's thinking about the spinal injury. The heart issue. They told her that you flatlined. Twice. While en route to a hospital in Germany from some undisclosed location. And this was a week after it happened." The strain in Evelynn's voice was almost too much to bear. "What you fail to understand is that Mom didn't hear that they brought you back, what she heard was that her son had died."

He glanced at his watch. A few minutes after five. Time for a beer. He meandered into the kitchen and ducked his head into the fridge. "I wasn't making light of Mom's feelings. But I passed all the physicals required of me for this job. The heart doctor says my ticker is doing great. That I'm as healthy as a horse. My lungs are strong. And as far as the rest of me goes, I know I have limits. I know I can't do what I used to. But some of that comes with age. I'm not running around getting shot at anymore. I'm a park ranger. I'll use my medical training out there on the trails if that's never needed. I'll deal with unwanted critters. And use my charm to help stranded ladies."

"Oh my God. Only you would go down that road," Evelynn said. "Speaking of which. Have we met anyone? Because I know you and while you might say you're on a sabbatical from dating, it's been a while, and you never go too long."

"I've been here one night, so not really." He plopped down in the recliner. The furniture that came with the place wasn't horrible. But it wasn't all that great either. When it came to discussing his love life—or lack thereof—with his sister, he always treaded lightly. It wasn't that he held back or didn't trust Evelynn, because he did. But she wanted for her big brother to be happy, and for her, that meant marriage and kids.

"What does that mean exactly?"

He took a healthy swig of his beer. "I'm not sure," he admitted. "I met a woman last night who happens to be my next-door neighbor."

"Oh, goodie. I'll get to meet her."

"Maybe not. She's only here temporarily."

"And that makes her all the more appealing to you," his sister said with a huff.

"Actually, it doesn't and that weirds me out a little." He fiddled with the label on the bottle. "She's got her own set of baggage."

"Sounds like you learned a lot about this woman in a single night. Did something happen?"

"Not like you think," he said. "We just talked. More like she got drunk, and I listened."

"Oh shit. You are a sucker for a drunk girl with problems and that almost never ends well for you because that's the wrong girl to fall for."

That wasn't a false statement.

"Is the baggage the problem, or do you like this chick more than you want to? Or both?" his sister asked.

"I have no idea," he said softly. There was something about Winslet that tugged at more than his heartstrings.

"Uh-oh. Is that bleeding heart of yours kicking in? Do I need to worry about you becoming a knight in shining armor? Because that never works out for you."

He chuckled. "I'm not going to try to save her." But he wasn't about to turn his back on her either and that was where he got himself in trouble more than once. It was how he ended up with Kiki and Becky.

"You have a kind soul when it comes to women who have problems and need help. What's going on with this one?"

*Knock. Knock. Knock. Knock.*

He jumped to his feet. The pounding at the door wouldn't stop. He glanced through the peephole. "Hey, sis. I've got company. I'm going to have to call you back and it might not be until tomorrow."

"We are not done with this conversation. You better not blow me off."

"I won't." He ended the call, stuffed his phone in his back pocket, and yanked open the door. "Winslet? What's wrong?"

She threw her tiny frame at him, wrapping her arms and legs around his body.

"Humph." He stumbled backward. His knees felt nothing. His metal hip, same. The other one, well that was an entirely different story. The muscles in his shoulders burned. His spine grappled to understand the strain that was just required of it. Quickly, he found his footing, kicked the door closed, and eased back onto the sofa.

She buried her face in his neck. He couldn't describe her tears as sobs. More like faint bursts of blubbering. If there was such a distinction.

"Are you hurt? Do I need to go get my medical kit?"

She jerked her head back and blinked. Tears rolled down her cheeks. "Excuse me?"

He brushed them away with his thumbs. "I was a combat medic. I'm a qualified EMT. The fire department wants me to volunteer. I don't leave home without my bag." He shrugged. "Now, are you injured, or are these tears from something else?"

"Can I just cry for a few minutes?"

"Yes." He pressed his lips against hers softly. Mistake.

She shoved her tongue into his mouth on a search

and destroy mission. It was anything but aggressive. It was wild and out of control. Certainly not what either of them needed in the moment.

"Nope. We're not doing that." He cupped her cheeks.

"You started it." She sniffled.

"I guess you can blame me for that." He tucked her face back into the crook of his neck and held her close.

When she sighed again, her body shivered.

He adjusted her on his lap, holding her tight to his chest. He ran his hands up and down her arm and back, letting his fingers get tangled in her long locks. Ten minutes ticked by and not a word was spoken. But her sobs had softened. Her breathing had returned to normal.

"I'm sorry," she whispered.

"You have nothing to apologize for." He tilted her chin. "Care to tell me what that was all about?"

"I called Shamus. He's coming to town. With his wife and kids and he wants to make sure me and my friends will help keep his dirty little secret—a secret." She blinked out a few more tears. "When I learned I was the other woman in this love triangle, that was a hard pill to swallow. I mean, I couldn't say he was cheating on me with his wife. It was always the other way around. That's what has made this so hard. And that jerk has not once apologized. Not even when I called him tonight. If I had known, I could have either decided not to get involved or been the other woman.

But it would have been a choice. He never gave that to me and now I'm reduced to this gross thing he did that he has to hide under a rug. Do you have any idea how that makes me feel?"

"I can only imagine." He cupped her beautiful face. He couldn't decide if he should be his usual sarcastic, inappropriate self and say something ridiculous in hopes it made her laugh.

Or be serious.

He held her gaze for a long moment, contemplating his words. His sister would tell him to be himself. That if any woman couldn't handle his dry sense of humor, she wasn't the woman for him.

But he wasn't looking for a woman.

His mother would tell him to be softer. Kinder. To think about how his words affected others.

"You look constipated," Winslet whispered.

"That's because my mind is." He dropped his forehead to hers. "My initial reaction to this dilemma goes something like this." He cleared his throat. "At least you have a boyfriend now to rub in his face."

She cracked a slight smile. "That's a little bit funny."

"But that doesn't really help you through this tough time, now does it?" God, how he wanted to kiss her again. But this time he wanted it slow. Controlled. And not because her emotions were all over the map. "Listen, just because he made a bad choice, that doesn't make you a dirty secret. That's on him. You're a beautiful, intelligent, witty woman who has more going for her than he'll ever understand. Don't let his inability to see you for who you really are stop you from moving past what he did."

She scooted off his lap, grabbed his beer, took a small sip, and scrunched her face. "I want to hurt him. That might not be right. But I want to see him suffer."

"I think that's a normal reaction." He took the brew back and swigged.

"Maybe so, but I don't want to hurt his wife or his kids." She dropped her head back and closed her eyes. "Especially his kids. I know what that's like."

"What do you mean?"

She rolled her head and curled her legs up on the sofa. "My father cheated on my mom. They're still together. I have no idea why she stays, because that man can't keep his dick in his pants."

"You really do call it like you see it, don't you?"

She nodded. "Don't get me wrong, I love my dad. He's not the worst man out there when it comes to being a father. He came to all the important stuff. Supported me. Did all the things a dad was supposed to do," she said. "I don't know if it was because of all the whispers about his dad killing his mom and running off with the neighbor or not, but ever since I can remember, my dad has cheated on my mom. I've caught him and it destroyed me."

"Did you tell your mom?"

She nodded. "She cupped my chin and had the nerve to tell me I didn't know what I was seeing and to forget about it. I tried to argue with her, but she shook her head and told me never to speak such nonsense again. So I didn't. I know he still cheats, but we don't talk about it."

"I understand now why this is affecting you at your core," Jett said. "Unrelated question, but I kind of have to know. Who raised your dad? I read that he was only fourteen when the murder took place, but I didn't get much further."

"Poking around in my background?"

"Just fascinated and Weston was telling me about it."

"My grandfather's brother," she said. "Not many people know this, because it was kept from the public, but Weston knows. My great-uncle Xavier was a suspect for about five minutes. Rumor had it he was having an affair with my grandmother. It was a pretty solid rumor and he and my dad never got along. But his uncle wouldn't turn his back on my dad. They've always had a weird, but adversarial relationship." She shrugged. "Seems this is a thing with my family and I'm just perpetuating it. Must be in the genes."

He waggled his finger. "Don't do that. And next time you have the hankering to call Shamus, come bang on my door before you do it. And if he calls you, don't answer it unless I'm within shouting distance."

"Aw, aren't you the sweet fake boyfriend." She let out a long sigh and stretched out her legs. "Thanks for letting me fall apart. Again. I promise you, this is not how I usually am. It's just that when Shamus and I were together, he never hid his affection for me. At least not around my friends. I didn't have to lie about him being my boyfriend to that small circle. The only weird thing he did was withdraw at any place he was teaching. That was the only time he preferred our colleagues not know about us. But most places had rules how we conducted ourselves romantically." She narrowed her stare. "And he never introduced me to his parents or siblings. We would make plans, but something always got in the way." She smacked her forehead. "God, I was so stupid."

"Let's stop going down that road." He took her hand and kissed it. "I'll cook us a nice dinner and we can chat about how to deal with Shamus' visit. Outside of my work schedule, I can make myself available for whenever you need me."

"You don't have to play *the boyfriend*."

"I know you've got a lot of friends in this town, including your girlfriends I saw you with last night." He took a calculated risk and pressed his mouth over hers in a gentle kiss. She tasted like peaches and cream. Sweet and dreamy. He could easily allow himself to get lost in the moment. But it wasn't the right time. Perhaps there never would be. He leaned back, holding her gaze. "We already set the stage with Shamus to have me around. I don't mind. I want to be there for you."

"Why? You barely know me."

"Sixteen months ago, when my helicopter went

down, Zeke got on a plane and flew to Germany. He didn't have to do that. But he was at my bedside for what seemed like forever. He stayed with me during my darkest hour. He held my mother's hand. He helped my sister and my dad with all the arrangements, making sure I had the best doctors. When I was finally stable enough to be flown back to the States, he was right there with me. I don't know if I could have survived without his support." He palmed her face. "Zeke cares about you. Therefore, I care about you. Not to mention Weston and I go way back. They are like family. I'm not going to leave you to deal with this alone. It's that simple."

"You military guys really stick together," she whispered. "I appreciate it, but I don't want to put you in an uncomfortable situation, especially one where you have to lie."

"It's not that big of a falsehood." He arched a brow. "Of all the women in that bar last night, I noticed only one. Only one who turned my head. Only one I would consider asking out. To be totally honest, I want to take her out on a real date." He'd lost his ever-loving mind. Getting tangled up with Winslet had disaster written all over it.

His sister was right.

His savior complex was coming out in spades.

But he had been attracted to her before he knew a single thing about her past. About her problems. That had to mean something.

"Now you're being a dork."

"I'm being honest," he said. "Shall we consider this our first date?"

"How about we see how the night goes, and I'll decide at the end."

"Fair enough." His sister was going to have a lot to say about this one.

# CHAPTER FIVE

Winslet stared at the backside of Jett while he finished the last of the dinner dishes. He was a fine specimen of a man. Broad shoulders. Narrow hips. Thick muscles everywhere. It was hard to believe that a few months ago, he was recovering from his final surgery on his right shoulder. Not to mention everything else he'd gone through.

She swirled her wine. Her stomach was finally willing to accept the alcohol. Not that she wanted to consume very much. She had been nursing this one glass all night. She might consider a second one, especially since the night had been more relaxing than expected, which was unnerving for other reasons.

Their conversation flowed naturally as if they were old friends who hadn't seen each other in years. Not two strangers getting to know one another.

It was weird but not uncomfortable, and that scared

her. The last thing she needed was a man in her life. Even temporarily. She could never live in Fallport permanently again, even if she loved the damn town and it checked all the boxes.

The local university had offered her a position. One that would allow her to continue her work with the FBI. She loved working on criminal cases. More than she enjoyed archeological digs. When she'd been younger, those excited her because of the travel and all that she learned. But now, as she approached forty, she wanted something different out of life.

Unfortunately, Shamus showed her that, and she resented him for it.

As much as she loved her parents and wanted this to be her safe haven, the place she came when life kicked her in the ass, being around her parents only reminded her of everything she'd allowed Shamus to steal. Being around her father, knowing of his betrayals, made her want to shake her mother.

It also created this desire to tell Shamus' wife.

But that wasn't her place.

She wanted coming home not to feel like a mistake. Only right now, her entire existence had become worse than a bad made-for-TV movie.

Jett would undoubtedly be a nice distraction from her problems. However, that wouldn't be fair to either one of them. Not to mention she could already see his fatal flaw. The one that made him appealing and made her want to run out of his apartment as fast as she could, all at the same time.

Most people built their greatest strength around their biggest weakness.

Jett had two.

He was the kind of man you could rely on. She suspected he was his family's rock. That if someone needed him at three in the morning, he didn't ask why, he just did what needed to be done.

But he never asked for a damn thing in return.

Strength.

Weakness.

Not because he was too proud or didn't believe he needed help. No. He didn't see it that way because he didn't have to. He had a few friends like Zeke. He'd been blessed that way, and it sounded like he had a strong family.

His second strength was that he was incredibly insightful—of others. But that was built out of not being so insightful of himself until it was too late. That took turning the lens inward and it wasn't something she believed he ever had to do very often. Not that he came off as if he were the golden boy of anything. However, his ability to accept life on life's terms wasn't because he learned some hard lesson—though he'd had many. It was because he'd been taught there wasn't a point in fighting it.

Perhaps that was true.

But if she lived that way, she would have never

gotten her PhD simply because most in her path told her she'd never be able to do it.

She rarely accepted no for answer.

He seemed to accept whatever life tossed at him.

"I love food, but I hate doing the dishes." Jett dried his hands, turned, and lifted his wineglass.

It surprised her that he had such an expensive taste in wine and a wide selection of it. He seemed more like a whiskey and beer man, but looks were always deceiving. Something her job and life had taught her.

"Not my favorite thing to do either, which is why I order out more than I eat in. Besides, cooking for one sucks."

He nodded. "My ex-wife loved to cook. Loved everything about it, along with being a housewife. She hated it when I was late and more so when I didn't text or call that I wouldn't be home on time. She was rigid about dinner. It was weird. I tried to tell her not to start it until I got home and then I'd help, but she had this old-fashioned idea that she wanted me to walk in the door and have it on the table."

"That's actually quite sweet."

"At first, it was. But it became stifling." He curled his fingers around his neck. "Like she had a choke hold on me. We fought about it all the time. There was no compromising with her."

"Seems like a strange thing to be so passionate about." She held up her hand. "On both sides of the fence. I mean, to me, that's an easy one to solve."

"There was only one solution in Kiki's mind. And that was for me to make it home at precisely the time food was put on the table. In my line of work, that's not always possible."

"None of my business, but did you ever try marriage counseling?"

He tossed his head back and laughed. Hard.

"What's so funny about that?"

"To me, the things we fought about were stupid. She picked fights over not putting the salad bowls in the right drawer. It was never the big things, so I didn't know our marriage was in that much trouble." He held up his hand. "I get that makes me look like an ass, especially the day I came home from a mission to find her things packed. I was dumbfounded and suggested counseling before just calling it quits. That's when she informed me she was in love with someone else. She'd already checked out. She rolled her suitcase out the front door and told me the movers were coming the next day to get her things. The divorce papers were on the kitchen table."

"So you gave up."

"There was nothing left to fight for. She was with someone else." He shrugged. "I wasn't going to beg. It did take me a bit to get over the shock of it all. I'm man enough to admit I was hurt and getting over her was hard. While I know I made a lot of mistakes in that relationship, she didn't fight for us either."

"You're a very logical man."

"One of the many complaints my ex-wife had about me." He polished off his wine and poured some more. "I tried to be a little less pragmatic and let my feelings out more when it came to Becky, but she too thought I was cold and distant."

"I wouldn't say that about you. I find you to be warm and kind. But you do approach things very much like a cop would a crime scene."

"Ouch. Not something a man wants to hear when he's trying to date a woman."

She leaned back. Her stomach filled with butterflies. Not many guys could have that effect on her insides. She prided herself on being in control of her emotions at all times. It was rare that she ever let anyone see her break down. But she'd done it twice with Jett.

And he'd been so sweet on both occasions. There was no judgment in his eyes for what she'd done or how she'd behaved. Her drunken stupor didn't seem to bother him in the least. Nor did her cryfest. She appreciated that about him. She also valued his honesty. But while he shared parts of his life, he did lack emotion, and that rubbed her the wrong way.

Shamus had accused her of being reserved about her feelings at the beginning of their relationship. But he did a three-sixty when she turned up the heat.

"You're very open about your life," she said. "In the couple of days I've known you, I've learned a lot about you. Your childhood. Your sister and family. Your career. Failed marriage. A helicopter crash that nearly killed you and what you went through to be able to stand here on your own two legs. But you don't really get into the emotions that surround those events. It's like you're detached from it all."

"It's in the past. I don't dwell on what I can't change."

"But you have to feel something about what happened to you. Much of it has shaped your life. Who you are."

He took his glass, and then with his free hand, he took hers and lifted her from the chair. "I feel them in the moment. I adjust my life accordingly." He guided her to the family room and eased onto the sofa.

The moonlight filtered through the window, casting a warm glow, making for a romantic ambiance that couldn't be denied.

"Are you hung up on why I'm not more upset over my ex-wife leaving me? Or Becky?" He stretched his legs out on the ottoman and swirled his wine.

"I suspect you were upset, but the way you share your experience, it's like a dry textbook. Or transcripts of a court hearing without the human touch. It's hard to relate to monotone," she said.

He laughed, but it wasn't a funny, haha laugh. More of a sarcastic grunt. "After Kiki left, I drank myself into oblivion for six months. I was a useless human being. I was angry as hell. Mostly at myself for not seeing the writing on the wall and not trying harder to save my marriage. Hell, for not knowing we had bigger problems. I felt like a fool for having no idea she'd been seeing someone else for months while I was deployed. Trust me, I had a plethora of emotions circling around in my heart and soul." He lifted his wineglass and took two large gulps. He turned his head and stared out the window. The scruff on his face was more pronounced than yesterday. He scratched at it. "When Becky dumped me, it was the day after my hip replacement. I was in so much physical pain that I could barely see straight. The doctors had to deal with my lung and heart issues before they dared deal with my hip, spine, and knee problems. It was this delicate dance to decide which part of my body to fix first, if I could be fixed at all." He dropped his feet to the floor and abruptly stood, marching to the window, tossing back his wine like it was a shot of whiskey.

This was the most emotion she'd seen from him outside of being kind to her when she'd blubbered all over his shirt.

He was far from putting this in his past.

He was human after all and while she didn't want to see this man suffer, it oddly warmed her heart to know that he grappled with his humanity like she did.

Because they weren't all that different. She often viewed showing her emotions as being weak. She knew that wasn't true, but having grown up in this town, with all the whispers about her family, she had to learn not to let it bother her.

Even though it did.

Jett set his glass on the windowsill and turned. The pain in his dark eyes was unmistakable. "Becky destroyed me," he whispered. "I don't blame her for leaving me. I actually understand how hard it had to be for her in part because I knew that was one of her biggest fears about being in a relationship with me, but to waltz into that room, the morning after that surgery, and tell me that we were done. That she couldn't sit by my bedside and help nurse me back to health, well, let's just say it set me back."

As gracefully as she could, she stood and closed the gap. She rested her hands on his shoulders, raised up on tiptoe, and kissed his cheek. "I'm sorry."

He curled his fingers around her wrist. "I don't like talking about this. I can't change the past and stirring up feelings over it won't do anything other than put me in a sour mood."

She wanted to tell him it was because he still held on to a few tiny pieces of those situations. He'd locked them in his heart and used the intense pain those women had caused to guide his decisions, whether he was conscious of it or not. "I can't change the fact that Shamus is married and chose not to tell me. But it doesn't mean it didn't hurt. You have more feelings about your past than you realize, and those emotions still affect how you handle things. It's like you've locked all that up and now you approach dating, or even wanting to get into my pants, like a transaction."

"That's what you think I'm doing?"

"I believe you're a kind man who has a big heart, but you protect it with everything you have because you don't want to get hurt again." She let out a long breath, resting her head on the center of his chest.

He took her chin with his thumb and forefinger, tilting her head. His gaze bored into her like a freight train.

"You have this backward," he whispered. "It's not me I worry about. I don't want to be the cause of anyone else's pain. I have a decent handle on who I am, which doesn't include a third go-around at long-term commitment. So, if I come off as aloof, or even a little cold, it's not because I'm guarding my heart. It's simply because I want to protect whomever I'm dating at the moment."

He could tell himself that all he wanted, but Winslet wasn't buying it any more than she could lie to herself about what she wanted for her future these days. But she wasn't about to argue with the man. It was his life. His heart. His soul.

His lips brushed against hers in a soft, slow kiss. He was a master when it came to kissing and she caved to her desire by wrapping her tongue around his, searching, demanding all the passion he could give. Her body needed it.

But her mind kept reminding her of all the reasons she should stop this insanity.

Sleeping with Jett would be about the worst idea she'd ever had.

Somehow, the proximity of their bodies made it all the more difficult to heed her common sense. Jett was like a potent drug, immediately addictive and intoxicating. He pulled back for a moment, dark eyes ablaze with fervor. It was impossible to ignore the curling heat in his gaze or how his breath hitched slightly as he dared to venture further.

His fingers traced down her spine, causing Winslet to shudder. She gasped, clutching on to him for support as her legs turned to Jell-O. This was wrong, oh so wrong, but how could she deny herself this pleasure?

Jett's other hand nestled gently in her hair, his lips returning to hers with an insatiable hunger. The world around them seemed to fade away. It was just him and her, entwined on this thin line between right and wrong.

A whispered plea escaped Winslet's lips as she guided his hand to where she needed him the most. Her heart pounded wildly in her chest as anticipation coursed through her veins. The voice in the back of her mind was now a distant echo, drowned by the symphony composed by Jett's hands, mouth, and body that played on her senses.

Despite knowing that this could be a disaster waiting to happen, she cast caution to the wind. "Shall we take this to your bedroom?"

Jett's eyes flashed with a dangerous glint, predatory and possessive. Without a word, he scooped Winslet into his strong arms, carrying her through the dimly lit hallway to his room. She nestled into his warmth, the steady rhythm of his heartbeat lulling her fears to silence.

Every nerve in Winslet's body tingled as he laid her gently on his bed. His broad shoulders blocked the faint glow from the moonlight outside, casting him in an ethereal shadow. His lips moved against hers once more, his taste a potent mix of wine and spices that set her senses aflame.

She reached up, tugging at his shirt. He lifted it over his head, revealing a chiseled chest lined with unspeakable scars. The sight of him was unforgettable—raw power contained within human flesh and then tortured with the scars of devastation and destruction. She instinctively reached out to touch him, trailing her fingertips across the raised skin. "What's this one from?"

"Heart surgery." He lifted her hand and kissed her palm before placing it on his shoulder. "I had two surgeries here and one on my other arm." He twisted his body, showing off a snakelike line that curved across his side and then blended into a long scar that went all the way up his spine to the base of his neck.

She swallowed. Hard. He'd told her of the crash. Of all the problems. Replacements. And the metal in his body. But nothing could have prepared her for this.

Or for how it didn't seem to faze him.

With a soft smile, he brushed away a loose strand of hair from her face, his touch surprisingly gentle. He lay next to her, fiddling with the hem of her shirt. "I'm sorry if they bother you, but there are many more. My hip. My knees. However, to me, they're reminders," he murmured, "of battles fought and won. Sometimes, I need to remember not only the struggle but the lengths it took me to get here."

Winslet's eyes retraced the scars, mapping out each ridge and hollow with newfound reverence. She laid her head on his chest, hearing the rhythmic thump of his heart, a testament to his fight for survival. Sitting up, she straddled him, ripped off her shirt, and flung it across the room.

A deep groan vibrated from his mouth and landed on her skin. Quickly, he unhooked her bra and brought his lips to her nipple.

A shiver of pleasure ran along her spine, her body responding to him in a way it had done for no other man. He kissed his way down her stomach, his hands traveling up her sides before resting on the dip of her waist. He touched her with care and slow precision, which belied the scars that marred his skin.

"Your body is..." He paused. His dark eyes met hers, shining with an emotion she couldn't quite decipher. "Perfect," he finished, the word barely more than a whisper. The scars on his back rippled as he pulled her closer to him, their bodies fitting together like two pieces of a puzzle meant to be connected.

"I'm not..." Winslet started to protest, but the rest of her words were swallowed as his lips silenced her. This wasn't about perfection. It was about acceptance, about feeling seen and valued despite—or perhaps because of—their flaws.

His hand traveled down her back, tracing the curve of her spine as he deepened the kiss. In a frenzy, they removed the rest of their clothing as if their bodies were on fire. As passion flared between them, Winslet forgot everything else—forgot his scars, forgot the past that had brought them to this moment. All she knew was him, every inch of him that fit so perfectly with every inch of her.

She moved against him, letting out a soft moan as his hand tightened on her hip. They moved together in perfect synchrony until time seemed to lose all meaning—a dance as old as humanity itself.

Her fingers scratched along the jagged scar across his shoulder, and he winced slightly but didn't stop moving. She paused and he gave her a brief shake of the head. "Don't," he rasped, "they don't hurt—but you make me feel alive."

And so she continued touching him, every scar, every imperfection, feeling his breath hitch and hearing sounds of pleasure escape with her touch. She created a map of his body from his lips. Each scar a story, each sigh a victory.

And there, beneath the sheets, bathed in the soft glow of the moonlight filtering through the thin curtains, they discovered each other's bodies and souls. They found solace and affection in one another's arms in a world of so much pain that had been inflicted.

But it wasn't going to save either of them from themselves. It didn't change her situation, and it wouldn't heal his broken heart.

He flipped her to her back and thrust himself deep inside. She accepted him as if that's exactly where he belonged. As if he'd come home. It was a sensation that startled her more than the climax that exploded from her body, causing a ripple effect of a second... and then a third.

She dug her fingernails into his back. "Oh God, yes," she whispered. The tidal wave of pleasure that curled her toes and swam across her skin right to her eyeballs had been nothing like she could have imagined.

And she felt his release slam into her like the ocean rolling over the beach.

His voice, barely more than a raspy murmur, muttered her name again and again as if it was a prayer or an incantation. She felt his shuddering sighs against her skin, the tremble of his body over hers. The raw power that had driven him only minutes ago, now melted into a tender surrender. His fingers traced over her face, lightly tracing her lips as if she were the most delicate of treasures.

He collapsed onto her, momentarily leaving her

breathless until he rolled off, drawing her into his arms. Their legs tangled together in a knot of warm skin and content sighs.

In silence, they lay in postcoital bliss. Winslet knew there was no turning back from this point—she had tasted him, felt him in ways she never thought possible, and succumbed to the intoxicating allure he had over her. There was no place she would rather be than in his arms.

His thumb brushed against the soft curve of her lips, causing them to part in a small sigh as she nuzzled deeper into his side. He kissed the top of her head.

As the moon slid along its nocturnal path, they held each other close under the warmth of shared covers. The room lulled them into another rhythm now—one of slow breaths and quieter whispers shared beneath the cover of shadows and silk sheets.

"I hope you plan on spending the night," he whispered.

Winslet looked up at him and knew without a shadow of a doubt she was in trouble and in more ways than one. "I don't think I could leave even if I wanted to," she admitted, her fingers tracing lazy circles on his bare chest.

He chuckled lightly, but a note of seriousness crept into his voice as he said, "Good, because I don't want you to, but you might boogie on out of this bed when I mention something that we didn't discuss before we let things get out of hand."

She rested her chin on his chest. "I'm on the pill. I probably should have mentioned that, and we probably still should have used something else for other reasons."

"Well, I'm glad one of us was being responsible because being a father isn't on my agenda."

That statement wasn't going to make her hightail it home, but now that her world had been turned upside down by Shamus, she knew without a shadow of a doubt she wanted more from life, and she wasn't going to get it from Jett.

He tilted her chin and kissed her tenderly. "Good night, Winslet."

"Sleep well, Jett." She rested her head on his chest and closed her eyes. The semester would be over in a month. She wouldn't bother staying through the summer. Her parents would give her shit, and she had nothing lined up, but she'd land on her feet.

She always did.

# CHAPTER SIX

Jett jerked awake. He blinked as he reached for his cell.

"What the hell is that noise?" Winslet asked. "And why is it going off?"

Freaking six thirty in the morning. He was going to have his sister's head on a platter and drizzle it with fish guts. "It's the ringtone I use for my family."

"It's horrible. You could have picked anything, including a song, but no, you chose the damn alien thing." She brushed her hair from her face and glared. "I was in the middle of a good dream, too."

He chuckled, tapping the green button on the screen. "Go back to sleep." He kissed her temple as he pressed the cell to his ear.

"I plan on it."

"Sleep? I think not," Evelynn's voice bellowed from his phone's speaker. "And who's the chick with the sexy voice?"

He let out a slow breath as he swung his legs to the side of the bed, found his boxers, and hiked them up over his hips.

"I can hear you breathing. Are you going to answer my question?"

Gently, he closed the door behind him and strolled toward the kitchen. "Why the hell are you calling me at this hour on a Sunday?"

"Andy had hockey practice and Carli has a game an hour later. I'm going to head over right before the puck's dropped."

"Since you're not coming down until after school gets out, I should fly up and watch the kids play. I miss those rascals, but it doesn't really explain the early morning call."

"Only a couple of weeks left of spring league," Evelynn said. "No point and stop avoiding the topic. You slept with her."

"You're the one avoiding and don't sound so shocked." He snagged a mug and set it under the machine.

"I kind of am. I thought we were going to ease into life in Fallport. Not ease into bed with the first girl who tickled your fancy."

He glanced down the hallway. "Yeah, well, shit happened." He tapped his fingers on the counter, waiting for the coffee to finish pouring into his mug. He didn't want to get deep into this conversation while sleeping beauty was ten paces down the hallway. He snagged his brew and headed outside, where he copped a squat on the front step.

"Talk to me, Jett. Last time you got involved with a woman, she tore your heart to shreds."

"You're exaggerating."

"Seriously? I'm the one who sat with you while you cried like a fucking little baby after Becky left you."

"I was more upset over the things she said about her brother. Not dumping my sorry ass. He was a friend of mine." Jett blew into the dark liquid. He wasn't in the mood for this conversation, but he knew his sister. She wasn't going to let him hang up the phone and not at least go through the motions. Besides, he did have a few lingering feelings about what the hell he was doing with Winslet that he needed to chat with someone about.

And it couldn't be one of the guys.

They'd all kick his ass.

"I understand that," Evelynn said. "And so not the point. You got involved with Becky right after she'd been in an abusive relationship. You were there for her when she needed a shoulder to cry on and you're always that guy. You never fall for the girl who doesn't need your help. Or shall we talk about Kiki and what she was going through when you first started dating her?"

"No. I'm well aware of my faults." He took a large gulp of his coffee, wishing he hadn't since it burned the roof of his mouth. He set his mug on the step. "I didn't intend for this to happen."

"Right. She just landed on your dick."

"Don't be crude."

"I'm being honest," Evelynn said. "And I'm sure she's a nice enough girl. They always are. Now, tell me her baggage so I can talk you out of this."

"It's a little too late for that. Even if she hadn't spent the night, I already agreed to help her with a situation."

"Of course you did." Evelynn let out an audible sigh. "One of the things that makes you so damn lovable is your bleeding heart, but it's the same reason why you can't find the right girl."

"I'm never going to settle down."

"Never say never," Evelynn said. "What turned your head with this one?"

He chuckled. "Well, it wasn't her problems. I didn't learn about those until after I was already thinking about her, if that makes you feel better."

"It doesn't, but at least I know you were thinking with your penis first and not your heart."

"That's the dumbest thing I've ever heard." He shook his head. "Most people would want it the other way around."

"Not if they knew your track record. So, what is it this time? Is she broke? Got a kid she's battling custody for? Parents who hate her life choices? And please don't tell me she's just off a bad relationship, because if this is another Becky situation, I'll be on the next plane down there to bitch-slap you."

"It's not exactly the same." He pinched the bridge of his nose. "There's no violence involved, so no need to worry about me getting in a fistfight." Hopefully, though he wasn't sure how he'd respond to Shamus if he was ever left alone with the man. While Jett could control his fists, he often couldn't control what came out of his mouth.

Not when it came to men treating women badly.

He might have been a shit husband, but he never raised his voice, or his hand, to Kiki.

He glanced over his shoulder. "I feel bad breaking her confidence about this, so you have to promise me this stays between us."

"As if I've ever broken your trust."

"True," he said. "Unfortunately, she spent eight months in a relationship with a man who was married, only he neglected to inform her of that status. To make matters worse, he has kids. Now he's coming to town and expects her and the few friends she has with her, to keep it all hush-hush, so he doesn't get caught. So he can go on with his life as if nothing happened. While she's dealing with a broken heart."

"In your arms."

"We had sex. Why are you making this weird?"

"Because I know you and you always fall in love with a woman who needs a strong man."

"You haven't met Winslet. She's not the kind of

woman who needs a man to take care of her. That's what makes this so hard," Jett said. "She's a lot like me. One short-lived relationship after the other. Never wanting anything too serious. Certainly not marriage or kids. But this guy she was involved with, she fell madly in love with, and it changed everything. Her entire world view, and now she's grappling with him coming to her turf. She wants to hurt him, but of course, she doesn't want to harm his kids. She knows what that's like. All I'm doing is offering friendship."

"And your bed."

He laughed. "I'm attracted to her. She's nice and incredibly hot. But she's not staying here longer than a few months. After that, she's gone. But once this guy comes to town, I get to play boyfriend."

"You've got to be kidding me."

"It's not a big deal. It will make it easier for her and perhaps help her move past all the hurt," he said. "And truthfully, it's helping me too."

"Oh yeah? How do you figure that?"

"Because I realized recently, I'm not completely over Becky." It took a lot for him to admit that out loud.

"You don't want Becky back, do you?"

"She said a lot of hurtful things the day she broke up with me. But I have no idea what I'd do if she showed up at my front door with an apology."

"Jesus," Evelynn muttered. "I can't believe I'm going

to tell you this. She reached out asking where you were a few weeks ago. I wouldn't tell her."

"You should have told me." His sister didn't keep many things from him, but when she did, they were usually big, and she always thought they were for his own good.

But they never were.

"If you wanted to talk to her, you could have given her your new cell number. But you didn't. And she's no good for you. I don't know this Winslet girl, so I can't make a judgment, other than she's a damsel in distress and that's never good for you. But I think I'd rather you take your chances with her than go back to Becky. Who breaks up with a man in a wheelchair?"

He opened his mouth, but his sister didn't give him a chance to respond.

"Oh, wait. I know the answer. A woman who didn't love you in the first place, that's who. And don't you dare go into all the shit about what a struggle it was for her dealing with you being deployed. She knew the score when she started dating you. Or how hard it was for her when you *died* and had to be brought back to life, because I'm your fucking sister. Trust me, I know what that was like. And the reality is, she wasn't as concerned about what happened to you, as she was the fact that she lost her brother."

"Now who's being dramatic," he mumbled. "Do me a favor and give Becky my number. If she wants to talk, that's between me and her."

"At least you're not asking for me to give you hers."

"I already have her number, but I'm not reaching out first. I don't owe her an apology. Actually, I don't owe her anything at this point. But I would hear her out."

"Fine," Evelynn said. "But over my dead body are you taking that woman back. She doesn't love you, Jett."

"I hear you." And he did. But that didn't change the unresolved sensation that swirled in his gut. Or maybe it was that he honestly needed closure. He needed to hear her voice to know it was truly over—for him. "Now, I do want to talk to you about Winslet." He reached for his mug and took a small sip. "I get that I have a pattern when it comes to women. I spent a few months discussing that with a therapist while recovering in that rehab facility. I don't want to fall into the same pitfalls with Winslet. Thing is, I do like her, but I need to figure out what is my so-called savior complex and what is normal male animal attraction."

"It's pretty simple. Have sex with her, don't try to fix her and her problems with her past relationship. Stay the fuck out of that one."

"Kind of hard when I agreed to make myself available to be her boyfriend around this guy when he comes to town."

"Only my brother would get involved with a woman who is in love with someone else," Evelynn whispered. "Okay. How about don't sleep with her again and just be her friend. Think you can do that?"

"I don't know. She's the kind of chick you wouldn't kick out of bed. She reminds me of Janice."

"Oh Christ. Why do you always have to bring up the one time I had a thing with a girl?" Evelynn said. "I was twenty years old. I was in college and experimenting. Sowing my wild oats. Besides, Doug was dating that god-awful woman. Hell, they were practically living together. I was bored. One could say I was waiting for him to smarten up and realize he was in love with me, though it took him long enough."

"Sometimes I think Doug wanted to have both you and Janice."

"What is it with you men?" Evelynn said with an ounce of sarcasm. "You know, he once asked me if I had pictures of us. That's so gross."

"He's a guy. And we're all visual that way."

"Oh my God. You're my brother. I can't believe I'm even having this conversation with you," Evelynn said. "Listen. I get you want to help this woman. It's kind. Neighborly even. I can even get on board with you finally getting yourself back out there. You haven't been with a woman since Becky. But when we do finally make it down there, I don't want to have to be spending it with you all mopey because some girl broke your damn heart again."

"I'm not going to fall in love with her. I've learned my lesson."

"If that were true, I wouldn't have woken you both up this morning."

He lifted his gaze and watched a couple parallel park their SUV in front of his building. The man raced around the front of the vehicle and helped the woman from the passenger side of the car. Her hair was cut short, to the shoulders, but she had a familiar look.

The shape of her face—with her high cheekbones and rounded chin—looked a little too similar to Winslet's. Not to mention the eyes were identical.

"Hey, sis. I've got to run." He stood, opening the door for the couple, painfully aware he was shirtless and shoeless.

The older gentleman eyed him suspiciously but nodded with a weak smile while his gaze still landed on the center of Jett's chest.

Right where the scar from heart surgery was located.

Jett knew the damn thing was right out of a horror show. It didn't bother him. Nope. It was a reminder he wasn't dead. He wore his scars like a fucking badge of honor. He'd decided that when the time came, any woman who couldn't handle them, well, they could walk right out the bedroom door.

Winslet hadn't even flinched. She appreciated them for what they represented.

His personal war with life and death.

One that he'd battled hard and won.

"Thank you," the woman said, lowering her gaze, trying to not to look, but she blinked. A few times. And it was impossible to miss how her eyes shifted right back to his scars.

"Call me in a couple days and I definitely expect to hear from you if Becky reaches out," Evelynn said.

"Will do. Love you, sis."

"Right back at you, big brother."

He ended the call and strolled inside, glancing over his shoulder. The couple stood in front of Winslet's door. The older man tapped his knuckles on the wood panel.

Well, shit.

Stepping across his threshold, he made a beeline for his bedroom, only to find Winslet hiking up her pants.

She caught his gaze, wearing only her jeans and a lacy bra. "My fucking parents are here. I guess they called and texted me last night and this morning. So did my sister, though hers was late last night."

"I believe I let them into the building."

"You did what?" She yanked her shirt over her head. "And they saw you walk into this apartment?"

"They did." He arched a brow. "I guess now they will see you come out of it." His heart thumped in his chest. Meeting parents wasn't his strong suit. He glanced down at his torso and all the scars that he knew must have horrified her parents.

No one in his family paid them any attention

anymore. Not even his mother, and she could cry at the drop of a hat when some people brought up the helicopter crash. But to everyone, the scars on his body also represented the fact that he was alive and breathing, something they were all grateful for.

"They have their panties in a twist over something," she said.

"At seven in the morning? On a Sunday?"

"They are on their way to church. Probably want me to go with them. But that's not happening. Could have to do with my little sister, Tammy."

"Of all the things we discussed, you never mentioned a sister."

"Because she's married to my ex-fiancé's best friend. They do everything together and while I'm over him." She held up her hand. "I really am. I don't like Harvey's wife. I don't like how Anne is now besties with my little sister and they do everything together and I'm just supposed to forgive and forget that Harvey dumped me three days before my wedding." She arched a brow. "I know I sound bitter. It's not about the relationship; its only about the fact my sister doesn't understand how awkward that is for me. Not to mention my father once had an affair with Anne's mother."

"You can't make this shit up." He inched closer, wrapping his arms around her waist, heaving her to his chest. "Does Tammy know about your father's infidelity?"

"I have no idea. She's six years younger than me. When I found out, I was fourteen. And Tammy has always been my father's favorite. She could never do anything wrong in his eyes. Me? I'm the girl who had a lesbian love affair in high school that shamed the family."

He burst out laughing.

She cocked her head.

"Sorry. But I was just talking to my sister about her little fling with a chick. Her husband used to ask her for pictures of it. Kind of cracks me up."

"I like your sister, but her husband is such a typical guy, and don't you have something to say about that? She's your sister. You should be defending her honor."

"My sister can fend for herself, and Doug was my best friend before hooking up with Evelynn. Besides, I've seen you naked. You should see the wild things going on in my brain right now. And it's all about you and a—"

She covered his mouth. "Men. You're all the same."

He curled his fingers around her wrists, leaned in, and took her mouth in a hot, wild, but brief kiss. "It's every guy's fantasy. But right now, it's being cut short by your cell going crazy over there."

"Yeah. I better go see what my folks want." She stepped around him and made her way out of the bedroom, through the kitchen, and toward the front door.

He followed. He shouldn't have. It was nuts. But he did it anyway. He reached around her and turned the knob.

She glared.

He shrugged as he pulled open the door.

Her parents turned. Her father cleared his throat. "Winslet," he said with a dark tone.

"Hey, Dad. Hi, Mom. What brings you by at such an early time?" She stepped into the foyer of the building.

Jett chose to keep the door open and leaned against the wood frame. He nodded, still aware he was shirtless.

Stupid not to put on a shirt.

"We tried texting and calling, but you didn't answer," her father said. "Where's your sister?"

"I would assume at home with her husband and child." Winslet planted a hand on her hip.

Jett should really excuse himself, but he was like a doe in headlights.

"We thought she was coming here," her mother said, clutching her purse for dear life. "She mentioned she might come over last night."

"She does know the code." Winslet scooted past her parents and pressed her fingers on the keypad.

"Are you saying you haven't been home all night?" her father asked, glancing between Winslet's apartment and Jett. If looks could kill, Jett would be underground.

He scratched at the scar on the center of his chest.

"That's really none of your business, Daddy." She

pushed open the door and groaned. "Well, there she is, sound asleep in my bed." Winslet tugged the door and sighed. "Why did she feel the need to sneak into my apartment and crash for the night?"

"No offense, but this is a family matter," her father said.

Jett raised his hands. "None taken."

Winslet leaned against the wall. "What's going on? Why didn't Tammy sleep at her own home last night?"

"We're not going to stand here in the hallway with your flavor of the month—"

"Daddy, that was rude," Winslet said.

"I've been called worse." Jett waved his hand. "If you want, we can all go inside, grab a cup of coffee, and wait for Tammy to wake up."

Winslet pushed from the wall and inched closer. "Thanks, but I'll go wake up my sister." She rested her hands on Jett's shoulders. "I'll call you later."

Without really thinking too much about the people in the hallway, he cupped her face. "I got a text from Zeke a bit ago inviting us over to his place for a barbeque around four, if you're interested."

"I'll let you know." She raised up on tiptoe and kissed his cheek. "I'll see you later." She turned on her heel and marched herself back toward her apartment.

Jett waited until she and her parents disappeared inside.

"Well, that was weird," he mumbled as he closed the

door. Part of him wanted to forget all about what might be going on with Winslet and her family.

It wasn't his business.

But unfortunately, his heart and soul actually cared for Winslet, as crazy as that might seem.

Yeah, he had issues.

# CHAPTER SEVEN

Winslet hated it when her family invaded her space. She much preferred to go to her parents' house, or even her sister's, for family gatherings. That way, she could leave when things got too weird.

Like now.

She knew her little sister's marriage wasn't perfect. She'd known that from the start. But it wasn't a bad marriage. They had a solid foundation despite everything.

Bennett had been Harvey's best friend since grade school. They had done everything together. They might as well have been brothers.

And Bennett had covered up Harvey's affair.

Something Winslet couldn't ever forgive him for.

But outside of that, Bennett was a stand-up guy. He was good to Tammy and a damn good father.

Tammy had only been sixteen when Winslet and

Harvey were to be married, and it had pissed Winslet off that Bennett, a grown man, had been eyeing Tammy. It didn't matter that he'd waited for Tammy to turn eighteen before asking her out. He'd been sniffing around her for two fucking years.

A second point that had gotten under Winslet's skin.

Tammy had been a kid. An impressionable teenager with a massive crush and Bennett knew that. He'd dated two other girls while waiting for Tammy to turn legal, making it even grosser in Winslet's eyes.

But to her parents, Bennett, much like Harvey, had been the cream of the crop. A good man. A decent man. One worthy of their daughter's affection.

Well, Harvey had turned out to be a two-timing cheater. But Bennett had not. He did love Tammy. But they had their issues.

He gambled. Not a ton. But it did cause a rift in their marriage. A few years ago, it had been a big enough problem that Tammy had given him an ultimatum. The last time Winslet spoke at any length with her sister about the issue, Bennett had gone to counseling and he'd been dealing with his demon.

He hadn't gambled in over two years.

God, Winslet hoped that wasn't the problem.

Tammy took the mug of coffee, palmed it, and continued to stare into it while she curled up in the bed. Winslet sat next to her, not sure what to say or even what to ask.

Their parents sat on the love seat.

Talk about a dysfunctional family.

Tammy, the good child. The one who did what the family expected. She taught grade school. The perfect profession for a young mother. One that allowed her husband to be the bread winner and if and when a second child came, she could give it up without a second thought.

Because it didn't matter.

At least that's how her parents thought.

Tammy almost never ruffled feathers.

She went to the college that her parents had picked out, instead of doing what Winslet had done, and that was—God forbid—thinking for herself. Her parents thought her career was strange. Who studied dead bones? If anyone should do that, it was a man, and even then, it was still an odd thing to do.

They could all go fuck themselves.

"What happened?" Winslet couldn't stand the silence anymore. "Why are we all gathered in my tiny studio apartment?"

Tammy turned her head and glared. "If you had answered my call last night, Mom and Dad wouldn't have joined us."

"And why did they? How did they even know you were here?" Winslet asked, though her tone could have been less aggressive.

"I don't know," Tammy whispered, shifting her gaze.

"How did you guess I would be here? It's not like this is my go-to place."

"Because we called your friends," Winslet's father said. "Your husband is worried about you. It's not like you to leave home. You have a child for Pete's sake. What the hell has gotten into you?"

Oh shit. "Bennett didn't have you come here?" Ignoring her parents, Winslet took her sister's hand. "Is he—"

"Dad? Mom? Can I be alone with Winslet for a minute?" Tammy asked.

"No," Winslet's father said. "What you need to do is go home to your husband."

"Excuse us for a minute." Winslet jumped to her feet. She jerked her sister off the bed. "Help yourself to more coffee. I also have breakfast fixings. We'll be back shortly."

"Where do you think you're going, young lady?" Her father was on his feet. He sported a scowl. The same one he had when Winslet told him she was going far away after she'd been jilted.

"I'm not all that young," Winslet said. "I want a word with my sister, alone. She came here to talk to me, and that's what we're going to do. You can stay, or you can leave." The one thing that Winslet had that Tammy didn't, was the balls to stand up to their father.

But that's because Winslet held the power to crush the man.

And he knew it.

"I will not be spoken to that way by my own daughter." He glared.

"I'm sorry, Dad. But I think Tammy has something she wants to say to me without the two of you hovering. Isn't that correct?" She squeezed her sister's hand. Again, they hadn't been all that close.

But they were still sisters.

That meant something.

Tammy nodded. A tear dribbled down her cheek.

"We'll be back." Winslet raced the five paces toward the door. She jerked it open and headed right toward Jett's. A dick move, but he'd understand. She pounded on the wood frame.

It opened five seconds later.

"Hey. What's going—"

She pushed past him, dragging her little sister behind her. "Jett. This is Tammy, my sister."

"Nice to meet you," he said with a little chuckle in his tone.

"And who are you?" Tammy asked.

"I think your dad referred to me as the flavor of the month." Jett shut the door.

"My father can be an asshole," Tammy said.

Winslet cocked her head. "I have never heard you refer to our dad like that."

"Come on. Are you going to deny that you know he cheats on Mom?" Tammy waggled her finger at Jett's mug. "Can I have a cup?"

"Sure." Jett nodded. "Are you hungry? I was just about to make some eggs."

"Starving. Thanks." Tammy plopped herself down on the sofa. "He's cute."

"Don't deflect. And how do you know about Dad?"

Tammy rolled her eyes. "Since right before you were supposed to marry Harvey. Like he was being all that discreet with Anne's mother. Please. I was going to talk to you about it, but you did what you always do and disappeared."

"That's not what I do." Winslet pursed her lips.

"Right. You hightailed it out of this town so fast it made my head spin. I was in high school. I had no recourse and Mom, she's a blubbering idiot who puts up with it. I even confronted her about it."

"You've got to be kidding me." Winslet took both mugs that Jett offered, handing one to her sister, and made herself comfortable on the couch. "Why didn't you tell me?"

"You took off. You made it clear that I was Daddy's little girl. That's a tough thing to be when Daddy's a prick."

"I'm sorry. I thought I was protecting you from the insanity of it all."

Tammy waved her free hand. "No. I get it. I'd probably do the same thing if I was the older sister. And I didn't make it any easier since I was madly in love with Bennett, who happens to be Harvey's best friend. Our dynamic isn't easy, but I would like to change that."

"So would I." Winslet swallowed the lump in her throat. "What's going on with you two? What happened to make you show up at my place, use the code to get in, and not tell anyone?"

"He didn't cheat, nor is he gambling, if that's where this is going." Tammy sucked in a deep breath and let out a long sigh. "But it does have to do with that shit of a best friend he has."

"What has Harvey done now?"

"You know his wife is pregnant with their third, right?"

"I heard that." Winslet nodded.

"Well, he might have also knocked up Ivy Palmer." Tammy arched a brow. "I don't know if you remember her or not. But she was on my dance team. She now owns a ballet studio in town."

"Oh. I remember her, all right. You and she were not friends." Winslet laughed. "You hated her."

"No. She hated me. But that's beside the point. The whole entire thing is so gross I want to vomit, and Anne has the right to know her husband is dipping his dick in someone else's vagina. I told Bennett I wanted to tell Anne, and he thinks I should keep my trap shut. He reminded me of how our mother doesn't care, and maybe Anne doesn't care either. But what if Anne doesn't know? I mean, once you found out, you kicked that asshole to the curb."

Just then, Jett appeared with plates full of food.

"Here you go, ladies." He set the breakfast on the

coffee table. "My sister has always told me I have a special talent for interjecting my thoughts where they don't belong, so before I go and do that, I'm going to ask permission to speak freely."

"That means you've been listening," Winslet said.

"Kind of hard not to. My apartment isn't that big." He sat in the recliner across from them and had the audacity to wink.

"I'm all ears." Tammy smiled.

"Take it from a man whose wife cheated on him. Knowledge is power, but the source does matter. If whoever tells her is coming from a place of love, it will be taken that way, even if she doesn't want to hear it."

"I struggle to believe that." Winslet took her plate and shoveled some eggs into her mouth. She chewed frantically before finishing her thought. "My mother didn't want to listen to me."

"You had skin in the game. You were angry. But also, for whatever reason, your mom is willing to live the charade. I know a few women who are more than happy to go down that road." Jett stretched out his legs and crossed his ankles. "You also have to remember that cheating isn't always about love. Or even sex. Or about what might be missing in a relationship. I know my ex-wife cheated out of boredom. Not because she wasn't loved. Or because she was missing something in the relationship. Although, I wasn't the warmest of men. But my sister learned she cheated in her next relationship, and I should have known she'd cheat on me since I was the other man before that." He arched a brow. "There are habitual cheaters. And there are cheaters who are looking for something. Sounds like this Harvey guy is of the former."

"He was dating someone else when we hooked up," Winslet said. "Made me feel kind of gross because he'd promised me they had been broken up at the time, but there was crossover."

"You made my point." He lifted his fork and shoveled more food in his mouth.

"That only makes me hate Dad and disrespect Mom more." Tammy scrunched her forehead. "Bennett and I fought because I'm pregnant again and he thinks for the sake of our family, I need to keep my nose out of it." She pointed her finger at Winslet. "Mom and Dad don't know about the baby yet, so please don't tell them. I'm so not ready for the onslaught of judgment about my life choices. Or both of them telling me how Bennett and I should raise our children. I mean, Mom thinks I didn't breastfeed long enough and that's why my toddler is chunky. Does she not remember what a fat little kid I was?"

"I would not call you fat." Winslet cocked her head. "A dork. Yes. But fat. No. And my lips are sealed," Winslet said with a smile. "I'm happy for you. I know you were trying for another one."

"Thank you." Tammy brushed her hair behind her ears. "Bennett is willing to distance himself from Harvey. But then there is the problem of our father. I can't keep my mouth closed any longer. I'm so angry. Bennett and I have had our share of problems. He's worked so hard to stay away from gambling. He doesn't even play in weekly poker games with buddies. He knows it could be the thing that lulls him down that slippery slope and I'm more important. However, it's an addiction. He has to work at it and if he ever went back to it, well, that could destroy us. I love my husband and respect him even more for not only putting his family first but doing the painful work to get himself back on track. I just don't understand why Mom stays."

"I think I should remove myself from this conversation." Jett stood.

No way was Winslet going to let that happen. She leaped from the sofa. "No." She curled her fingers around his thick biceps. "You have an opinion. You lived some of this and you know all of my story. I want you to stay and I think I can speak for my sister as well."

"Yeah. I agree. I want to hear from the flavor of the month too."

"Seriously, Tammy?" Winslet glared. "I don't think Jett likes being reduced—"

"It's fine." He chuckled. "Considering the circumstances. There are worse things one could call me." He cleared his throat and flopped back into the recliner. "Tammy, may I ask you a couple of difficult questions?"

"Sure," Tammy said.

"Is this the first time that you know of that Harvey has cheated on his wife?" Jett asked.

Tammy glanced at her hands. She fiddled with her fork. "Well, no. And that's honestly part of the problem. I'm tired of being a secret keeper. While Anne isn't my bestie, she's still a friend. It's hard for me to look her in the eye, especially now that we're pregnant at the same time. My oldest and her middle child are the same age. They are in the same preschool. It's the whole girl code thing. And Bennett, he's torn. He knew about Anne when Harvey and my sister were together and said nothing and to this day has guilt over that. He hates being put in that position but doesn't want to be the one to come out and say it. We're in a horrible situation no matter what we do."

Winslet took her sister's hand. The fact this was the first time she was hearing all this broke her heart. She understood much of why Jett approached his life with such a pragmatic view. It was easy to see why Winslet could be at fault for part of her and her sister's lack of communication and lack of closeness over the years.

So much misunderstanding. So many lies. Half-truths.

"What I'm about to tell you must remain in the vault of sisterhood," Winslet said.

"Oh my God," Tammy whispered. "You haven't said that in years. It scares me."

"It shouldn't but still. I don't want Mom and Dad knowing about this. It will only cause a bigger rift in our relationship. But it might help you understand a few things." She squeezed her sister's hand, holding Jett's gaze, hoping for a dose of courage.

Which she got in spades.

"A few months ago, I was in a relationship with a married man," Winslet said softly. The shame of the words smacked the center of her heart like a category five hurricane.

"I find that hard to believe." Tammy's eyes grew wide with shock.

"Your sister didn't know he was married." Thank God for Jett and his kind words and sweet voice. "He lied to her their entire relationship. When the truth came out, he expected her to hide it. Sweep it under the rug like a dirty little secret."

Tammy gasped, covering her mouth. "How horrible."

"It was," Winslet admitted. "Only it gets worse. He and his family are coming here, and I'm expected to keep quiet."

"You don't keep quiet about anything," Tammy said softly.

"I will about this because he has kids." Winslet took her sister's chin with her hand, much like her mother did all those years ago, only the intent was much different. "When I learned about Daddy and his affairs, I went right to Mom. But she acted like it didn't matter. That I needed to hush my mouth. That I didn't know what I'd seen or heard. Maybe she was trying to protect me. You. I have no idea. But as much as I want the man I had the affair with to suffer for what he did to me, to his wife, those kids are innocent. They love their father. They are small children and don't need my wrath. If he didn't have kids, I'd probably find a way to tell his wife. But I'm not going to be a vindictive woman just because I can."

"But what if she came to you and asked? Would you lie?" Tammy stared at her with her mouth gaping open.

"Probably not," Winslet admitted. "But I won't go to her freely just because I want to cut him off at the balls. I'm better than that. I think you should stop hanging around Harvey and Anne. If Anne asks why, tell her to ask Harvey. Have Bennett back you on that. Push Harvey to be honest. It's not your place to tell Anne what he's been doing." She lifted her sister's chin. "No one told me, but the truth did come out. It always does."

"I can attest to that," Jett interjected.

"And what about Mom?" Tammy asked.

"She knows the truth about Dad." Winslet dropped her hand and sighed. "Mom either doesn't want to face it or it's okay with her. Either way, it's not our marriage. You need to focus on yours."

"I can't believe you, of all people, were in a relationship with a married man," Tammy said.

"Trust me. It wasn't by choice," Winslet said. "If I had known when I met him, I wouldn't have slept with him at all. I might not do long haul, but I do have standards."

Tammy turned her head. "And this one meets your standards?"

Winslet groaned. "I'm not answering that in present company."

"But I will." Jett chuckled. "I'm not married. Nor am I involved with anyone other than your sister at the present time. I'm not interested in marriage. Been there, done that. Don't really want to do it again. I believe that meets your sister's standards." He waggled his index finger. "I also didn't shy away from being called a flavor or from being mentally killed by your parents. So, I think for now, I'm within whatever your sister calls a *standard,* though my sister is currently contemplating boarding a plane, so she come down and check her out for herself, because she's not so sure Winslet won't break my heart."

"Oh. Trust me. Winslet will totally destroy your heart. But unfortunately for you, you won't see it coming."

# CHAPTER EIGHT

The first day on any job was like—well, Jett didn't know. He didn't consider any new position with the Army or Special Forces a new job. It was simply advancing his career.

Working as a ranger was something completely different. Some might consider it boring as hell, especially after coming from Special Forces, but Jett found it to be exactly what he needed.

Peaceful.

Refreshing.

He stood outside his post and stared out at the mountains and smiled.

He could get used to this.

The afternoon on the trails had been quiet. Not much had happened. Of course, it was April. The air was crisp and chilly since the temperature had shifted drastically in the last twenty-four hours. Not too many people ventured out this time of year—not yet anyway. Those who did find themselves hiking were diehards. They came out rain, shine, or snow. They wanted the exercise, the exhilaration. They wanted to push their bodies to the limit and come back for more. It wasn't about seeing the sights. Or sharing the experience with friends or family.

It was about the adrenaline rush.

That was something that Jett understood.

But his days of chasing that rush were over. He could appreciate watching others chase it for themselves. While he absolutely enjoyed hiking, which is why he took the job, he knew his body had more limits than he cared to admit. Like jumping from a perfectly good airplane. Those days were out of the realm of possibility, at least for the pure pleasure of it.

He supposed that if it came down to a life-or-death situation, he could.

But his role in life dictated that he didn't have to at all. And he had to admit, he liked it that way.

He set his water bottle on the railing and leaned against the wood, staring out over the vastness of Virginia. The massive mountaintops lingered in the distance, calling to his heart. The thumping of his pulse hit the center of his throat.

Yesterday, he'd gone to Zeke's barbeque alone. Winslet had opted to go to her sister's and spend time with Tammy and her family. While he understood, and supported her decision, he'd still found himself feeling a little lonely at the party.

Worse, when she'd opted not to show up at his place later. But he understood her reason. She hadn't graded any of the papers or prepared for her lectures. He didn't want to be a distraction from her career. He wanted to support it. That thought made him chuckle. When he'd first met Kiki, she worked as an office manager for a local marketing firm. To her, it was a job, not a career. Something she did to pass the time until she had children.

Jett didn't have an opinion one way or the other about whether his wife worked or not after kids came. Although, he wasn't in as big a rush as she was, but back then, he did want one or two. Once he and Kiki married, she surprised him by quitting her job. That had been quite the shock. He made decent money, so it wasn't as if he couldn't support his family.

But her income would have been nice. However, that wasn't even the biggest issue. It was the constant pressure to start a family and how she treated him. It was like they had walked right into a black-and-white movie set.

He sucked in a big breath, enjoying the fresh air.

This was the life.

The first two hours he'd spent between meetings and walking the terrain. Now he was lucky enough to spend the rest of the day out on the trails or in this post.

He was going to like this job. And Fallport.

A couple raced up the trail toward the hut.

"Hello?" The man waved his hand frantically.

Jett jogged down the steps. His new knees carried his weight with ease and no pain. But he felt a few twinges ripple up his back.

The doctors told him those would never go away. That some pain would be part of his DNA for the rest of his life.

All he had to say about that was it reminded him he was alive.

"Is everything all right?" Jett asked.

The woman held a good-looking dog on a leash. A mixed breed. Maybe American bulldog and shepherd, but Jett wasn't sure. He loved dogs and wanted to get one now that he was out of the military. He missed the one he'd gotten Kiki. Damn thing had been too stinking cute, but Kiki hated it and rehomed it.

"We're not sure," the man said, jerking his thumb over his shoulder. "Our dog, Boomer here, has this terrible habit of digging."

Boomer inched closer, sniffing at Jett's feet.

He leaned over and patted the dog's head.

"We're trying to break him of the habit, but it's not easy," the woman said. "Especially out here."

"Anyway, he was going nuts. When we got close to the area he was going crazy over, we saw something disturbing," the man said.

"And what was that?" Jett asked.

The woman hugged herself. "Bones and I just hope it's not human ones."

"Why don't we go take a look." So much for a quiet first day. "My name's Jett McCoy." He stretched out his hand.

"I'm Jon Montgomery, and this is my wife Harley," Jon said. "I know Boomer should have been on a leash, but he's a good dog. Friendly. He doesn't run off too far and there wasn't anyone on the trails."

"I'm not going to cite you for the leash law," Jett said. "But understand it's not just about the safety of others when it comes to pets being leashed. It's also for their safety. We have bears, cougars, and other animals that might see Boomer here as a threat or as food. He'd lose in that fight." Jett snagged his radio. "Ranger McCoy to base."

"This is base, go ahead," Chuck's voice crackled over the device.

"I'm headed south from my post on the red trail to check out a possible unearthing of bones."

"That sounds exciting," Chuck said. "I'll have the locals on standby and send Andy in your direction."

"Thanks." Jett clipped his radio on his belt. "Are you two camping or just out for the day?"

"Camping. It's our anniversary weekend and we do this every year." Jon took his wife's hand. "We had just packed up and were going on one last hike."

"Congratulations. How many years?" Jett had learned that in any high-level stress situation—though he wasn't sure he'd call this that—small talk was a great way to make people feel at ease. While Jon appeared to be somewhat unfazed by what had happened, his wife was as white as a ghost.

"This is five years, and we got lucky this year with the weather," Jon said. "Last year it rained, and it was freezing. My bride was not happy. I think she would have rather spent the weekend at a hotel, instead of here."

"The second night wasn't so bad," Harley said. "But next year, we won't be doing this." She glanced toward her husband and lowered her chin. "Camping will be saved for the middle of the summer when it's nicer. And we will be bringing the baby."

"Are you expecting?" Jett asked.

"She sprung that one on me last night." Jon pointed to an area off the path as he tugged at the leash.

Boomer wasn't happy. He yelped and dug his paws into the ground.

"Not that it was a total shock, but I was surprised," Jon said. "Boomer, knock it off."

"Congrats again." Jett stepped in front of them. "I'm going to need you to hang back while I go take a look, but before I do that, I have to ask a few questions."

"Okay," Jon said.

"What exactly did you see?" Jett glanced toward where the dog had been digging and obviously wanted to get back at it.

"We were coming up the trail. Boomer was ahead of

us. Something had gotten his attention," Harley said. "When we got closer, he was digging like crazy. We tried calling him, but he wouldn't come." She closed her eyes and sucked in a deep breath.

Jon wrapped his arm around her shoulders. "It's okay, honey."

She blinked.

"We both strolled off the path and Boomer lifted his head, all proud, and he had a bone in his mouth. I'm no expert. Hell, I'm a math teacher at the local middle school, but it definitely looked human to me."

"I have to ask. Did you touch it?" Jett would have been weirded out by that too.

"No." Jon shook his head. "I yelled at Boomer to release and lucky for me, he did. I leashed him right away and we came and got you."

The sound of boots hitting the hard dirt path caught Jett's attention. He glanced over his shoulder and waved at Andy. "Here's a colleague of mine. We're going to go check things out. Stay right here, okay?"

Boomer barked and tugged at the leash.

Jett met Andy about ten feet from the couple and explained the situation before trekking through the brush. "Damn, that dog can dig." He stared at a large hole in the ground. Next to it was the dropped bone. It looked like it could be a forearm.

He wasn't an expert either, but his best guess: human.

"We need to call this in." Andy took off his hat, scratched his head, and took a step back.

Jett leaned a little closer, but he couldn't see anything else.

"Our local police department won't be able to handle the forensics on this. They will call in either the Feds or State." Andy readjusted his hat and unclipped his radio. "Base, this Ranger Andy Wilber. We definitely have a bone. Appears to be human at first glance. If Weston Campbell is on duty, get him out here. Or his wife."

"Andy, this is base," Chuck said. "Weston is standing in my office and will head your way now. He's already called Police Chief Hill, who will contact Morgan with the State forensics team."

"Thanks." Andy clipped his radio back on his belt. "I bet this is not how you wanted to spend your first day."

"I could think of worse ways," he said. "I better get back to that couple and let them know what's going on. Weston's going to want to get their statement."

"It's going to get dark in less than two hours. It will take them one to get back to the parking lot. I'm sure they can do it down at the station."

Jett checked the time on his cell. He pulled up Weston's contact information and tapped the green button.

"Hey, man. I'm just about to hop on an ATV. ETA about twelve minutes," Weston said.

"Quick question. What do you want me to do with the couple that found the bone?" Jett had been prepared for a million different things that could have happened while on the job as a park ranger. Cuts. Scrapes. People who fell and sprained something or even broke something. Missing people. Fires. Any number of problems.

But this was not something he ever expected.

"I'll get their information when I get there, and then they will be free to leave," Weston said. "But I do have a bit of bad news. Morgan said removing any remains would be impossible because of how early it gets dark. He's not even sure he can get here before the sun sets, but he's going to try. That means we need someone to stay out there."

"I'll volunteer, no problem," Jett said. "I don't have a wife or kids, so it's no sweat off my back."

"State will put a couple of uniformed officers out there. We just don't have the manpower."

"I'll take what I can get. See you soon." Jett motioned to Andy, who was kneeling closer to the hole in the ground. "I'm going to radio Chuck and let him know that I can stay out here tonight."

"Thanks, man. My wife's eight months pregnant. She's uncomfortable as hell and I don't think she'd handle me being gone all night." Andy took a stick and poked at the dirt.

It was going to be one hell of a first twenty-four hours on the job.

* * *

Winslet closed her laptop, leaned back, and rubbed her temples. She loved teaching. Most of her students honestly wanted to be in her classroom. The study of anthropology—at least to her—was about as exciting as a roller-coaster ride. Add in forensics, and it really got her blood pumping.

Bones told a story, and it wasn't just about the person to whom the bones belonged, though that was an important piece of the puzzle. But when human remains were found, and the authorities had no idea what had happened, the bones had to be used as the key ingredient in finding those answers.

A tap at the door startled her. She glanced up. "Hey, Emory."

"Hey, yourself." Emory set a soda and a muffin from the cafeteria on the desk. "Thought you might be hungry."

"I'm famished. Thanks." She twisted off the cap of the beverage and brought it to her lips, guzzling down half of it before ripping open the package of the chocolate treat filled with preserves. "One of these days, my eating habits are going to find my hips."

"I seriously doubt that." Emory plopped herself down in the chair across from Winslet. "Guess who Sarah spoke to earlier today."

Winslet groaned. "If you're going to tell me she got a call from Shamus, I don't want to hear about it." Winslet had finally taken the time to look at the rest of the guest lectures, and Shamus had been on her calendar since the beginning of the semester, something she should have taken a closer look at. But it didn't matter. Nor did it change how she taught her course because, generally, each guest would talk to the entire department in the lecture hall, affecting everyone's schedule.

Shamus would be no different.

"She called him." Emory arched a brow. "She is the department head, and she confirmed his schedule. She's bristling with excitement over his arrival. She asked him about the dig the two of you were on and suggested that you present something together." Emory raised her hand. "I told her that you know what it's like to be the guest and you wouldn't dream of taking away from his talk, since he'd be focusing on a different aspect. As in his specialty, not yours. I also mentioned that we already covered it."

"Thanks for that."

"She scowled and mentioned he stated he preferred to give this set of lectures alone. She was hoping I'd speak with you and talk you into reaching out to him, suggesting he change his mind." Emory shook her head and laughed. "Remind me why we invited her out with us last weekend?"

"Because she's currently our boss. She's not the worst person in the world. And she overheard you, me, and Julie talking about it and felt left out. Besides, we've known Sarah for eight years." Winslet shuffled a few papers around on her desk. "She's pushing me hard to take a full-time position here. Sweetened the deal by saying you and Julie have jobs—outside of your role with me—and it wouldn't be a problem for me to work criminal cases as they came across my desk. She wants to set up a meeting within the next week or so to discuss the specifics."

"I heard ever since she got married, she's itching to have babies and be a stay-at-home mom." Emory patted her flat belly. "I got nothing against women who make that choice. My mom stayed at home and loved every second of it. She never got bored or felt trapped. But that shit is not for me. Wouldn't be surprised if Sarah's searching for her replacement—in you."

"I'd be an idiot not to entertain a department head position. That's a big freaking deal." Winslet clasped her hands together and rested them on the top of the desk. If her parents didn't make her so fucking crazy, she wouldn't even have to think about it, if that's what Sarah was offering. "But living in this town would be hard. Turns out, my father is screwing a girl who is only five years older than me. I don't know if I could be around that all the time."

"Jesus, that's gross."

"It's made worse by the fact her husband died six months ago and she lives in my parents' neighborhood."

"How do you know he's fucking her?" Emory asked.

"Because I saw them this morning, and then I got to hear a few people whispering about it. He also did his best to ignore me. As in pretend he didn't see me. He's so not discreet. It's pathetic. I can't even feel sorry for my mother anymore. And the worst part is, all it does is bring up all the stories about my grandfather. Did he murder my grandmother? Was he having an affair with Hannah? And then there's Cooper. He totally believes my father did it. When I was little, Cooper would sometimes come at my dad in town. But he never said the words out loud. Never actually accused him in front of me or my sister. Cooper would waggle his finger at my father and say something like *eventually, the truth will come out.* Or *how does your uncle not know what you are?*" Winslet sighed.

"It's still hard for me to believe that your great-uncle Xavier never really spoke out publicly."

"After the murder, Xavier focused his attention on two things. Dealing with my father and making a pest of himself at the police station. I've heard he might have been worse than Cooper. But he didn't accuse anyone. He wanted answers. I remember speaking with my uncle at length about the whole thing when I was working on my dissertation. He'd been devastated. His brother disappeared without a trace. His sister-in-law may have been murdered by his own flesh and blood. And he was left with a teenage boy who hated him because of the rumors." She chuckled, shaking her head. "My uncle and father never got along. I can't understand why because it wasn't my grandmother who was having the affair, but my grandpa."

"Neither one has ever given you a straight answer, have they?" Emory asked.

"Not really. Before my uncle's memory went, he would tell me that my dad struggled because of what happened. That he'd been traumatized and needed to direct his anger somewhere. My dad maintains that my uncle wasn't a nice man. That living with him was hell and the second he turned eighteen, he moved out. It's just weird. But it's like everyone in this town is waiting for history to repeat itself."

"It amazes me how quickly that case went cold," Emory said.

"You and me both." Winslet opened one of her drawers and pulled out a thick file. "This isn't even everything I have on what happened. There are more articles and theories written about the murder. But the evidence does point to my grandpa killing his wife. His prints were on the murder weapon. He disappeared. But the only thing that points to the affair between him and Hannah was that note." Winslet let out a long breath. "However, lots of other rumors surfaced about him being a horndog just like my dad and now I'm no better."

"Stop that. You're nothing like your dad and you know it." She arched a brow. "And just because you enjoy men and don't want a serious relationship in your life right now, doesn't make you a player."

"I want to fucking strangle Shamus. He could have said no to speaking at this university. He knows I grew up here and damn it, I confided in that man about my dad. He knew my issues about cheating, and he didn't have the decency to come clean. Nope. He had sex with me twenty minutes after I told that fucker."

"Yeah. He's a dick."

Her cell buzzed.

The caller ID was the state police.

"Hello. This is Winslet Payne." She tapped the speaker button.

"Miss Payne. This Morgan Rock with the State forensics team. You came highly recommended by my colleges over with the FBI and we have a case that we need your help on."

"Please call me Winslet, and I'm listening." She leaned forward, catching Emory's gaze.

"About two hours ago, a couple hiking just outside of Fallport found what we believe are human remains. It's too late now to dig them all up, so one of the park rangers and few state troopers will be securing the site and staying the night. But would it be possible for you to come out here first thing in the morning and give us a hand? And then work your special magic and help us find out who this is and what happened to them? I understand you're a professor at the local—"

"It's not a problem. My assistant can take over my classes."

Emory nodded.

"Thanks. A park ranger will meet you at the base at eight and bring you up to the location."

Quickly, she pulled up Julie's contact. "I'll be bringing one of my team members. Her name is Julie Hammel."

"Perfect. See you then." The line went dead.

"I see how this will be now that I'm pregnant." Emory waved her hand in the air.

"If you'd rather come, I can always have Julie handle my classes," Winslet said.

"God, no. It's fine. There will be enough to do once you get the bones back to the lab. I'm happy to go over the finer points of human evolution and other topics." Emory stood. "And perhaps I can get some intel on the Shamus situation. Like where he's staying and for how long."

Winslet nodded. "That might be helpful. That way I can avoid him at all costs."

"More like you can spend all your time with your sexy neighbor."

"Don't make me regret telling you." Winslet wadded up a piece of paper and tossed it at her best friend.

"I wonder if he's the one spending the night up there. Wasn't he working today?" Emory gripped the door handle.

Jett had texted asking her to call as soon as she could. But she had been in the middle of a class and needed to finish some paperwork.

"Today was his first day. He may be involved," Winslet said. "When is Oscar coming back?"

"He'll be here on Thursday, and thankfully, he's got

a few weeks of no travel." She pursed her lips. "I really don't want to bring this up in passing, but it is something we need to talk about."

"You're going to do that to me while standing at the door, ready to leave? You know I hate that."

Emory nodded. "It's just, now that I'm pregnant, I have to think about stability."

"You mean staying in one place." Winslet leaned back and sighed. "Where is it that you want to settle?"

"Oscar and I don't care where we live. His parents live in England and that's never going to change, and he doesn't want to go back. My parents are gone, and I have no siblings." Emory smiled. "You're the closest thing I have to family. But it would be nice to buy a home to raise this little one. We both like Fallport. It's a nice town. A great place to have a family."

"You want me to take the job." Winslet shouldn't have been surprised. It wasn't the first time she and Emory had this conversation. Only, in the past, it was a discussion of someday, way in the future.

Well, the future just smacked her in the face.

"I didn't say that. But right now, there are no other offers on the table. It's possible that in two years, one might open up in Colorado. We could stay here temporarily until that happens."

"I do have my name on a couple of lists." Winslet understood Emory's position. She had a family to consider now, and moving around all the time might not be horrible for a baby or a toddler, but it wouldn't be the greatest for a school-aged kid.

Now that Winslet had a major breakthrough with her sister, things did feel different.

And Fallport was her childhood home. She could admit that it still gave her a warm fuzzy feeling whenever she returned.

Until a rumor, or her father, mucked it all up.

That was always the thing that got in her way of taking this damn position, which would be a good career move.

"You know what, let's sit down and talk about this next week. We'll go over all the pros and cons and I'll really give it a real consideration."

"Winslet, I know you. And I love you like a sister. But don't offer to discuss something that in the back of your mind you know you're never going to do, even if the pros outweigh the cons. Thing is, I had to tell you what I was feeling, especially if Oscar and I decide to make a change."

Winslet's jaw fell open. She never expected to hear that from Emory's mouth. It was one thing to express concern and ask Winslet to consider a full-time job—anywhere other than Fallport. "Are you saying you'd quit?"

"I have a child to consider, and both Oscar and I are tired of living in rentals. We want a home. We want to plant our feet firmly in the ground and give our kid stability. So, yeah, quitting is an option."

Winslet pressed her hands on the desk and pushed to a standing position. She made her way across the office and took Emory's hands. "I want you to know that I heard every word. I really did. We've been through a lot together. I know I'm a little lost right now and this whole thing with Shamus has thrown me for a loop. But you, me, and Julie. We're a team. I will sit down with both of you and fully open my ears to what you think about this job offer and what you think the three of us should do next. I swear to you I won't make this all about me."

Emory leaned in and kissed her cheek. "That's all I ask."

"Have a nice evening. I'll call you from the bone site tomorrow."

"Be safe out there." Emory pulled open the door and strolled down the hallway.

Winslet made her way back to her desk and picked up her cell. Her chest tightened. Her heart thumped in her throat as if it were trying to jump out of her body. If she lost Emory, it would be like losing a body part.

No, it would be like losing her soul.

But damn, fucking Fallport?

Could she do it?

The truth was she could deal with the rumors about her grandparents. It was an unsolved murder, and people were going to whisper about it. She could join the conversation. Ask what everyone else thought.

That's what Weston did and he always told her it brought insight and color to the case.

But what she struggled the most with was her father and the constant reminders of how her life had turned out.

She tapped her screen and found Jett's contact information. Meeting him had been both a blessing and a curse. He was kind. Sweet. Sexy as hell. He was a good listener. He didn't judge.

But he made her feel things she didn't want to feel. He grabbed her emotions, put them in a blender, and let the top pop off, leaving her with a pile of confusion splattered everywhere.

Even though he could be warm and caring, he had this cold side to him. As if a big brick wall had been built around his heart.

That she could understand, based on his history.

She had one too. But he'd already chiseled his way inside. She wasn't sure there was anyone who could hammer their way through his.

So, why was she calling him now?

"Hey, Winslet. I was hoping I'd hear from you soon," his voice boomed through the speaker. The sound rippled across her skin like warm ocean water on a hot summer day. She told herself it was only because of the sexual attraction. Part of her felt bad, because she didn't like using people, and that's what she was doing.

She needed comfort. A safe place to land. Normally,

that would be Emory. However, right now, she was part of the conflict that swirled in Winslet's brain.

She could call Tammy. Their relationship had grown, and Winslet enjoyed the woman her little sister had become. But reaching out about all this might be too much and she didn't want to strain their delicate bond.

"Sorry it took so long for me to return your call," she said.

"No worries. I figured you were busy. I don't know if anyone has contacted you yet about the discovery out here."

"Yeah. The state police called."

"Weston told me they would and that you and your team would probably be out here in the morning. I was hoping you could stop by my place and bring me a couple of things since I'm going to be stuck out here all night."

"Text me the code and a list of things."

"Thanks. I appreciate it."

"It's going to be chilly tonight." When she'd been in high school, one of her favorite things to do had been camping. Even on a cold night. She moved toward the window and glanced toward the white moon. It wasn't completely dark yet, but the stars had begun to dot the evening sky.

"I'm used to it," he said. "Sorry I have to cancel our plans for tonight, but I'll make it up to you."

Perhaps she'd make it up to him.

"I'll see you later." She ended the call and snagged her bag from the back of her chair. She'd never minded being alone, but tonight, she didn't want to.

# CHAPTER NINE

Jett was no stranger to sleeping under the stars in the middle of nowhere on a cold and lonely night. He'd seen his share of dead bodies. Even had a couple of buddies die in his arms.

Those were the toughest.

And they haunted his dreams.

But this would be the first time he sat on a rock, roasting a hot dog over an open flame, next to an area roped off with crime scene tape where human remains had been found.

Life could be so much worse than this, something that was easy to remind himself of as his back ached with a constant dull pain that shimmied up his spine.

Through the sounds of the crackling fire, he heard the hum of an ATV on the access trail about a half mile away. He glanced at his watch. It was nearly eight in the evening, and he wasn't expecting company outside of the stoic state trooper who didn't seem to want to move from his post.

Not even for a crisp hot dog or some beans from a can.

It was better than the food he used to eat in the Army when he'd been on a mission, that was for damn sure.

His only job tonight was to make sure nothing got at the bones. That meant little to no sleep, something he was used to.

He stuck the hot dog on a bun and stared it, willing it to cool as his stomach growled like a grizzly. "Are you sure you don't want one?" he called to the trooper.

"I'm good. Thanks," the trooper said. "But it appears we might have company." He pointed toward the flashing lights down the trail. "Any idea who that might be?"

"Not a clue." He stuffed half the tasty treat into his mouth, chewing carefully. It was still fucking hot. "But there are a dozen occupied campsites on the first ridge and about the same down by the parking lot. Anything could have happened." It was twenty paces from the site of the bones to the main trail. He finished his meal and watched as two people approached. Shielding his eyes with his hand, keeping the light from blinding him, he tried to make out the figures.

One male.

One female.

No way.

"Winslet? Is that you?" He dropped his hand to the side.

"Thought you might like a few comforts from home." She adjusted a large backpack, gripping the straps with both hands.

"I told her she was nuts for coming up here tonight." Chuck shook his head and laughed. "I need to get back to the main office. I'm out of here at eleven. Andy said he'll be in early to check on you. Ronnie will be in the office at six, and Moose is on call."

"Thanks, man." Jett nodded. "But you can't be leaving her out here all night."

"Don't speak as if I'm not standing right next to you." She tilted her head and glared. "And I'm a big girl. I grew up in this neck of the woods and I've camped here more than you have." She planted her hands on her hips. "I think this might be your first time."

"She's got you there." Chuck laughed. "Besides, when this one gets an idea in her head, there is no talking her out of it. I learned that when she was my lab partner in chemistry." He waved his hand. "Have a nice night. Don't let the bedbugs bite."

"So, you and Chuck go way back, huh?" Jett reached out and lifted her pack off her back.

"He took me to the junior prom," she said.

"Should I be jealous?" He stared at the backside of Chuck, who was still laughing.

"Ask her about the limo ride and then decide how jealous you really want to be." Chuck glanced over his shoulder. "Still one of the best nights of my life, though every time Winslet comes back to town, my wife likes to remind me who I married. I enjoy that, so I milk it."

"You're lucky Renee and I actually like each other, because you can be a real asshole," Winslet said.

"No. I'm just a normal guy with a twisted sense of humor. One of the many things Renee loves about me." He waved the flashlight. "And why you dated me in the first place." He disappeared around the bend.

"Well, that was interesting and informative." Jett pressed his hand on the small of her back and led her through brush toward his small campfire. "I wasn't planning on pitching the tiny tent. Actually, I didn't even bring it from the cabin, and I can't leave to go get it."

"I'd rather stare at the stars and moon all night anyway. It's why I brought a nice warm sleeping bag." She leaned over the crime scene tape, tapped a small flashlight with her hand, and waved it around the hole. "I'm glad they didn't disturb the ground too much. I want to see how the rest of the bones—if there are any —are laid out."

"You're not going to start working tonight, are you?"

"No." She sat her cute butt on one of the rocks, lifted a stick, and poked at the fire. "I don't have any equipment and once I get in the zone, it takes forever to get me out."

"Good. Because I'd rather talk more about you and

Chuck." Jett considered himself a decent judge of character and Chuck seemed like a good man. The best.

Jett had met many of the men and women who worked at the ranger station. He enjoyed most. But he really liked Chuck. He was a bit of an oddball, but that was part of his charm.

"Chuck and his wife are two of the few people in this town who don't constantly look at me and think about what my grandfather did or what a shit my father is. We all went to school together. Renee and I were friends. Still are."

Jett set her pack near his things and joined her around the fire.

"Weird question." Jett found himself both oddly jealous of Chuck and totally intrigued by the humor he shared with Winslet over their past. Over the weekend, he'd learned so much about her family life and history with two of her exes, but realized, he didn't know enough about her at all.

He wanted to rectify that.

A thought that scared the shit out of him.

"How much time passed from when you dated Chuck and he got together with his wife?"

She tilted her head, and her lips formed a seductive smile. "I'm a little surprised you got hung up on that and not the limo."

He chuckled. "Oh, we'll get to that in a minute. Now answer my question, please." He eased down to the ground and stretched out his legs. The hard rock did nothing for his back. It was going to be a long and painful night.

In more ways than one.

Thanks to a state trooper only thirty paces away.

"I dated Chuck for about eight months. It started in the middle of our junior year and ended by the middle of the summer. Nothing tragic happened. No big fight. No cheating on either one of our parts. I think we were just young and not ready for something that serious. But we did have a lot of fun when we were together. That man is one walking sarcastic comment after the other. However, that's partly why I wanted to call it quits. That gets old. Renee loves him for it." Winslet glanced to the sky. "I believe they started dating when they were in their last year of college. They went to the same school. Were good friends. Then one day, they were a couple. A year later, they were married. And honestly, they are perfect together." She lowered her chin. "I will say this, though. Looking back, he was probably my most healthy relationship."

"Now I'm jealous."

She rolled her eyes.

"So, what happened in the limo? Did you lose your virginity to him or something?"

"Oh my God. What is it with you men and a woman's virtue? It's just sex." She joined him on the ground.

He inched closer. "First time is always the one we remember the most."

"Is that true for you?"

"Yes and no." He winked. "The other night was pretty freaking memorable. Not to mention incredible. But I'm not letting you off the hook. I have to work with that man. He's already got ideas in his head, since you made him drive you up here."

"He's got sex on the brain. Ask his wife."

"I'm asking you about the limo." He tapped his finger on her thigh. "Was that your first time?"

"I didn't have sex with him in that stupid limo. If you must know, he got a blow job."

Jett groaned. "I think that's worse, and I almost wish I hadn't pushed."

"Does that mean we're not going down the virginity road?" She folded her arms and glared. "Because I have to hear your story."

"The likelihood that you will ever run into the first girl I ever had sex with is slim to none. Hell, I haven't seen her since I left for West Point."

"That sounds like a story."

"Not a very good one," he admitted.

"Who was she?"

"Kind of the first girl to break my heart." Jett didn't too often think about Piper. He'd barely known her, but he'd fallen hard for the idea of her. And he carried her picture around like a lovesick puppy for months. "Come on. It's getting cold. Let's open our sleeping bags."

"Oh no, you don't. I told you—"

"I'll tell you." He took her by the hands. "But I'm freezing my ass off. How can it be hot during the day and freezing at night?"

"I brought you sweats and a long-sleeve shirt. I know I shouldn't have rifled through your drawers, but I thought you might be more comfortable sleeping in that than this uniform." She ran her hand across the center of his chest.

He wasn't sure how he felt about her taking that initiative. He didn't have anything to hide from her, but that was a big invasion of his privacy. He'd broken up with girls in the past for less.

But oddly, he wasn't too fazed by her actions.

"Thank you." He lifted her hand and kissed her palm. "Maybe we should zip our sleeping bags together."

She jerked her head. "Not with spying eyes over there."

"For body heat." He chuckled.

"That's what they all say."

It took about ten minutes to unroll their sleeping bags and change into warm clothing. Lucky for him, she took him up on his ingenious idea. Although, all that was going to do was torture him for the rest of the night. But it might help him stay awake. Something he needed to do.

She snuggled in next to him, resting her head on his shoulder, while he stared at the night sky. It was so damn peaceful. It comforted his aching soul.

Dying and being brought back to life was something he didn't remember happening, but it had changed him fundamentally. While he'd always been grateful for his life, his family, and everything else that had come his way, he'd never truly valued it until that day.

Every breath he took was new and exciting.

Every morning he blinked open his eyes was a gift.

One he wasn't about to piss away.

"I'm listening, or do we have to play twenty questions to get it out of you," she said.

He ran his fingers through her long, silky hair.

"Joining the military or going to West Point hadn't been a lifelong dream of mine."

"Then how did you end up there?"

"I'm a minus 1 handicap in golf."

She jerked to a sitting position, both hands pressed hard against his chest. "That is a shocking revelation."

"Why?"

She palmed his face.

He'd always grown facial hair fast and hard. He was well on his way to a full beard.

"I don't know. You don't seem the country club type."

"But I grew up on one and I grew up with a golf club in my hand. However, when I was a little boy, I wanted to be on the soccer team. Sadly, I kind of sucked at the sport. However, golf was something that I did for fun in the summer. I loved going with my dad.

And by the time I was ten, my mom would drop me off at the course and I'd stay there with my friends until it got dark. I never thought anything of how prestigious the course was I grew up on. It was just where me and my buddies hung out. Although, I did understand that there was a dress code and rules and all that." He tugged her back to his chest, circling his arms around her body. She fit perfectly.

"Sounds like a privileged life."

"It was," he admitted. "By the time I was a sophomore in high school, the coach told my father I could go to any division one college I wanted to. That I could legit get a scholarship. But then something weird happened. My dad ran into an old buddy, who happened to be a professor at West Point. When they showed interested, it piqued my curiosity. I went and visited, and I was all in."

"This is fascinating, but what does it have to do with your first time having sex?"

"I was a bit of a late bloomer, and I wasn't much interested in having a girlfriend most of my teenage years. My mom at one point was sitting around waiting for me to come out."

Winslet covered her mouth and giggled. "I'm sorry, but you are so far from gay. Not that there is anything wrong with that."

"Nope. There's not. Anyway. It was the summer before I left for West Point, and I met this chick. Her name was Piper, and she was smoking hot. She worked the pool grill at the country club. It was taboo for her to date the members. I flirted with her. Hard. But she was like, nope. No way. However, I finally got her to agree. We went out a couple of times, but I was weeks away from leaving and I really didn't want to go to West Point a virgin. That felt like not only the kiss of death, but I thought where would I ever find a girl, much less the time."

"Oh my God. That's the most pathetic thing I've ever heard. Please tell me you didn't use the line about going off to some battle zone."

"No. But we're not allowed to leave West Point that first year. And I really liked Piper. I told her I'd write and she could come visit. That we'd figure it out. I mean, it was her first time too. And it was so awkward and clunky for both of us."

"I hope you got a second chance to prove it gets better."

"Nope. She started avoiding me. Mind you, it was only ten days before I left. But she kept coming up with excuses." He shifted so he could see Winslet's beautiful face. "I wrote her every chance I got, and she wrote me only one letter, which I received around Christmas."

"What did it say?"

"Basically that she wished she'd never been with me. That she was sorry, but it was a mistake and she had to tell me, and then she begged me to stop writing because she was seeing someone else."

"Damn, you know how to pick them," she whispered. "What did you do?"

"What do you think Mr. Pragmatic who doesn't show a lot of emotion did?"

"Dove into your studies, golf, and lived your life."

"Pretty much." He took her mouth in a hot, wild kiss. It crackled like the flames of the fire reaching for the moon hanging low in the night sky.

She broke it off long before he was ready. "Do you regret being with her?"

"I don't do regrets," he whispered. "So, no. I don't. I mean, there are things in my life I could have done better. I could have been a better husband. A better boyfriend. But I don't regret anything. If I did, or if I wished my life were different, I wouldn't be here under this magnificent blanket of stars with a beautiful woman in my arms."

"First. Wow. What a line." She smiled. "And second. I wish I had that attitude about my life because sometimes I can't help but have regrets."

"My grandmother, who is one of the most amazing women I've ever known, always told me that when we keep even one foot firmly rooted in the past or in our mistakes, we close ourselves off from the future and all the possibilities. She taught me that disappointments in life will never go away and that I needed to learn to embrace them. That with every one thing that doesn't go according to plan, something magical around the corner is about to happen. I have to say, she's been mostly right about the philosophy."

"She sounds like a great human."

"The best." He slipped his hand under her shirt, sliding it up her bare skin and cupping her breast over her lacy bra.

"I'm not going to have sex with you," she managed as her chest heaved with a deep, raspy breath.

"I'm not asking you to." He fanned his thumb over her nipple. "All you have to do is enjoy pleasure. Kind of like Chuck did in that limo ride." He winked.

"I never said other things didn't happen in that limo. All I said was we didn't have intercourse. And for the record, I never slept with Chuck."

"Good to know, because I might have to beat the shit out of him if you had." He unhooked her bra.

"This is such a bad idea."

"As long as you can remain quiet, it's the best idea I've ever had." He lifted her shirt and lowered his head, sucking her taut nipple into his mouth.

He lost all control when it came to Winslet, and she was right. This was about the dumbest thing he'd ever done.

But he wasn't about to stop.

Nor would he regret giving her pleasure.

She'd had enough hard knocks in life, something he also understood. Only his attitude gave him the ability to push past things differently. He knew his past relationships with women still affected him at the core. He knew without a doubt that his sister was right about him on all counts.

He had a savior complex.

He had this weird need to honor, defend, and protect. When he saw injustices in the world, especially where women were involved, he couldn't keep his nose out of it. That was only made worse when he was attracted to that woman, and he cared.

Like with Winslet.

His sister also told him that his heart had been wounded right out of the gate and because of his inability to truly allow himself to feel that pain deep in his soul, he'd never be able to fully give himself to a woman. A fact he'd finally faced after Becky had left him.

But Winslet made him want to feel everything.

He'd already told her things about himself he'd never really shared with anyone other than his sister. Talk about vulnerable. Winslet already held the power to crush him.

And somehow, he didn't care.

She was worth the risk.

Except, she wasn't going to stay.

Another thing Evelynn was right about.

He went for the kind of woman who wasn't totally available. The ones who either had so much baggage they couldn't see past their own problems or weren't willing to freely give themselves to him anyway.

He was a lost cause.

He switched to the other breast, enjoying her fingers in his hair as she massaged his scalp, encouraging the experience.

Tugging at the drawstring of her sweats, he eased his hand inside her panties. Her legs spread, giving him full access.

She moaned.

Now that, he was going to have to stifle.

He lifted his head and kissed her hard. His tongue swirled around hers in a search and destroy mission. He swallowed every moan as he inserted two fingers and his thumb rubbed against her nub.

She reached for him, but he batted her hand away. She tried again, this time cupping him and it was apparent she wasn't going to let him go.

"No," he managed.

She blinked. Staring at him with passion in her wild eyes.

"Yes." She tugged at his sweatpants, her hand slipping inside and her fingers grazing over his length.

He should stop this. But he couldn't—or wouldn't—he wasn't sure which one. It didn't matter. It was too late. He lifted his head. He couldn't even see the state trooper.

Which hopefully meant he couldn't see them either.

But they were inside a sleeping bag, which is where they would remain.

And he would cover her mouth if he had to.

Because she was a little bit noisy.

Which he liked.

Just not in this moment.

He rolled her pants over her hips, finding that sweet spot once again. He felt a sense of desperation for her body to rock with pleasure. To feel the heat pour out on his fingers. He honestly didn't need to be inside her to feel satisfied. Hell, he didn't even need to climax for that to happen.

All he cared about was giving her pleasure. Making her feel like a woman. Desired. Wanted. Cared for. As if she was all that mattered.

And right now, that was true.

He pushed her to her back, finding her nipple with his mouth, sucking on it hard, while his fingers danced inside her body.

Her hips rolled with the pressure of his hand. She gripped him. Gently at first, but as the pleasure in her body came close to being tipped over the edge, the pressure of her hand intensified, as did the stroking.

It drove him mad.

He needed her. Needed to be inside her.

Nestling between her legs, he thrusted deep, capturing her soft moans in his mouth as he kissed her sweet lips.

Her legs wrapped around his body like a cocoon. Her movements matched his own with feverish desire. She shuddered, digging her nails into his shoulders and arching her back.

His release came seconds later.

He continued to kiss her, slowly. Gently. Before nuzzling his face in her neck.

Her fingernails ran up and down his back as she let out a long sigh. "I don't want you to think this is why I came here tonight," she whispered.

"I don't. Not really anyway." He pressed his lips to her cheek and rolled to the side, pulling her close. "And even if it was the only reason, I'm not complaining."

"Of course not. You're a guy."

He chuckled. "Why did you come here?"

"I thought you might want company." She rested her chin on his chest. "And I didn't want to be alone."

He ran his thumb over her bottom lip. "Did something happen? Because if I didn't pick up on the cue that you were upset, I'm sorry."

"You can be a really sweet man." She palmed his cheek. "When the sun rises, and the town learns there were remains found up here, everyone is going to be wondering if it's my grandfather or maybe Hannah Wilks. I think part of me didn't want to face that. And the other part wants to dig into my job and find the truth, putting an end to it for good."

He pulled her as close to him as possible. He should have thought of that. God, he could be so inconsiderate at times. He pressed his lips against her temple. "Whatever you need from me, I'm here."

She sighed, snuggling closer.

"Get some sleep. And if you wake up and I'm not in

this sleeping bag, don't stress. It's because I'm technically working."

"Oh boy. Ranger Jett did a bad thing."

"I could never regret being with you for a single second." No matter what happened, Winslet couldn't be seen as a mistake.

Not even when it ended.

And it would end. He could feel how she had one foot out the door. It didn't matter that he knew she liked him. Might even care about him.

Her wall and wounds were just too big.

# CHAPTER TEN

"Thanks, Chuck." Winslet took the glass of wine that Chuck offered and took a big sip. The last four days had been the most grueling since she'd returned to Fallport.

Not even spending Christmas with her parents had been this hard.

And they could be brutal with all the fakeness on that holiday.

So far, the only thing that she knew about the bones that had been uncovered was that they were female. That the woman was approximately between thirty-two and thirty-five years of age. That she'd been shot in the chest.

Twice.

And that was not her original resting place.

But she needed a different kind of expert to help her with that, and the best in the field was fucking

Shamus, and the damn State Forensics caught wind that he was headed in this direction.

So, of course, they wanted to call him in to consult.

Even though he didn't do that often.

He'd had the nerve to text her with his travel plans. As if she cared when his plane landed or where he was staying.

"How are you holding up?" Chuck asked, leaning against the railing on his back porch. His two boys, ages eight and six, raced around the backyard while one of the teenage girls from the neighborhood played referee so the grown-ups could have a quiet evening without constant interruption from the kiddos.

Sometimes it was hard to believe that Chuck was married with two kids. Then again, he was a kind man with a big heart, even if others in this town saw something else.

"I've been hiding between my classes and working late in the lab," Winslet said. She wondered if she should tell Chuck about the job offer. Or that she was seriously considering it. Well, one minute she was, and the next she wanted to race to the airport and buy a ticket to anywhere.

Three things were keeping her in Fallport.

Two she was willing to admit.

Stability and Tammy.

The third one was complicated, and it scared the crap out of her because it was not only unexpected, but it didn't make sense. She worried Jett was a rebound.

Or that maybe she was one of the many women he fell for because they needed help.

That was a pattern, and she wasn't blind to it. Only, she really didn't need his help.

She desired his support.

Fundamentally, there was a difference, but she worried he didn't know that was the only thing she needed from him. Well, that and his... she would not finish that thought.

"And what exactly are we hiding from?" Chuck raised his beer and gulped. "I heard the latest rumor about your dad. I'm sorry, but she's young and this one feels grosser than some of the others."

"It's disgusting. I'd almost rather he go back to fucking only married women, which seemed to be his thing. But someone only a few years older than me who just lost her husband? Ew." She peered through the sliding glass doors. Leaving Jett alone with either Chuck or Renee could be a mistake. Didn't matter they were the only people in this town she called friends these days, they were ballbusters.

Both of them.

They could also be fiercely protective of those they considered in their inner circle.

"And it's so sad how he died," Winslet said.

"Death by suicide is always difficult. That one shook this town. Her husband was this bubbly guy. Smiled and waved to everyone. He was kind of a dork and I feel like a shit for poking fun at him."

"You couldn't have known."

Chuck nodded. "Bad segue, but you and the new guy?" He glanced over his shoulder. "That happened quick."

"I don't know what you're talking about. We're just neighbors and he's been quite helpful with everything." Winslet's cheeks heated.

"Right. It's me you're talking to. You know. The guy who drove you up to see him five days ago. The one who you called to make sure it was me on duty as to avoid the whispers from the peanut gallery." He poked her arm. "I understand privacy is important to you, especially in this town. But since when do you care what people think about your bed partners?"

Instead of responding to that statement, she opted to drink more of her adult beverage. It was a nice cab, and it went down smooth. She glanced at the sky. "Oh, look at the moon. It's so pretty."

"I'm not letting you avoid this. I know you, Winslet," Chuck said. "We've been friends for a long time. You're friends with my wife. We've shared a lot of things over the years. So, don't go getting all weird on me now."

"I just don't want to talk about it."

"Is this because of the married guy you were seeing that State wants to bring in?" Chuck lowered his chin and cocked his head. "Remember, if you tell Renee, it's like telling me. And vice versa. We don't have secrets. You know how she feels about that. And she told you she would share it with me anyway, so don't play dumb. It's not a good look on you."

Truthfully, Winslet wasn't upset that Renee had spilled the beans. Only problem was that Winslet herself had told too many people. It was one thing for her to inform the people that she and Shamus had spent time with when the affair had occurred.

But everyone else?

All that could lead to was someone getting in Shamus' face or telling his wife, and that wouldn't be good.

Especially for their kids.

She did honestly care about their well-being. They were innocent. They shouldn't be pulled into adult drama. But they also deserved two present parents. And they certainly didn't deserve to find out about their father the way she did.

It was a constant battle in her mind and heart about how to handle this situation. Winslet had no regrets in telling her mother. While it did put a strain on their relationship, at least her mom had the information. It was up to her to decide for herself as to what to do with that intel.

Winslet had no idea if Feya knew and that was the rub.

"It's not about Shamus. Although, I'm worried about him coming here and he arrives Monday. While I want to hurt that bastard for the position he put me in,

I don't want to hurt his family. Only problem is I'm afraid I'm telling too many people on purpose."

"I will never forget the day you and Renee found out that your dad was sleeping with her mother." He smacked his hand against his forehead. "I'm the only one who ended up with a black eye while trying to break you two girls up and still, all I can think about is wanting to pour Jell-O over you both."

"You're a pig." She punched him in the arm.

"I don't deny that." He chuckled. "Outside me, Renee, Emory, and Julie, who else knows?"

"My sister and her husband."

"Seriously?" Chuck shook his head. "I adore your kid sister, but that's a hot button for her. I don't know if you know about—"

"Oh, she told me and that whole thing is about to blow up, but it's not my problem," Winslet said.

"I feel bad for Anne, being pregnant and all. But honestly, she knows her husband has a wandering eye," Chuck said. "Did you tell anyone else?"

"I might have told Zeke, Weston, Tal, Brock, Ethan, oh hell, the entire group of those guys."

Chuck sucked in a long breath and closed his eyes for a couple of seconds before blinking them open. "None of them will say anything, but they aren't going to be warm and fuzzy with this man." He raised his hand. "I think you're trying to get someone to leak the information because you've always believed the wife, or husband, should be armed with the information."

"I have always maintained that position, but I was never the other woman. I don't want to be a home-wrecker."

"You've always been the kind of person who takes responsibility for your own actions. I admire you for that. But you didn't know when you started seeing him and he did lie to you." Chuck squeezed her forearm. "What happened when you found out he was married?"

"That was it. End of affair. I never saw him again. But that doesn't change the fact that he was a married man, and I was the other woman."

"Perhaps not. But let's be honest. You wouldn't have gotten involved with him if you knew. That's one hell of a big deal-breaker for you." He clanked his beer against her wineglass. "If his wife finds out and she leaves him, it won't be your fault. If you had stayed with him, I'd have very different words for you. I know you feel like you've done something wrong. But you haven't. Shamus is the only one to blame in this situation." He pointed toward the house. "I want to talk more about Jett."

Winslet rolled her eyes. "Why?"

"Because in all the years I've known you, I've only seen you jump into two relationships with both feet. Me and Harvey."

"Don't flatter yourself." She lowered her chin. "We were kids and more best friends than boyfriend and girlfriend."

"I'll admit that you and I wouldn't have gone the

distance. Not because we didn't care about each other." He laughed, shaking his head. "You were my first love. Sounds kind of weird to say that, but it's true." He waggled his finger. "You are way too good at redirection. Sometimes I think you should have been a lawyer."

She shrugged.

"My point is we went from zero to sixty in a second. You did the same with Harvey. But every guy after that, it was a snail's pace, or you were just having a good time. Even with Shamus, it took you a few months to open up." He rested his hand on her shoulder, giving it a good squeeze. "I know how that changed you. Why it changed you. It's also why I'm a little shocked to see you dive right into the deep end with Jett."

"You're reading too much into it." Except, he wasn't. He was right on the money and Winslet knew it. A fact that terrified her because the last thing she wanted was a broken heart.

Or to break his.

"Am I? I see the way you look at him. The subtle way you lean your body into his. Or the way your hand brushes over his shoulder when you walk by." He held up his hand when she opened her mouth. "And it goes beyond that. You've told him things you don't tell anyone. You've pulled him in deep. And I know he's done the same, and while he's an open book, he's not an emotional man."

"I wouldn't say that."

"You're making my point for me." Chuck lowered his chin. "Look. I like the man. He's a good person and good for you. But you tend to get weirded out when people accept life on life's terms. Jett is that kind of man."

Winslet didn't need Chuck to explain the kind of human Jett was or how Jett processed life. She'd seen and felt it firsthand. But Chuck didn't know the half of it. Or the wounds that were buried deep in Jett's soul. Jett could accept reality all he wanted, but he still needed to feel the emotions that lingered in his heart.

And he had a few.

"Dad, can we go down the street to Timmy's house?" Brodie asked. "A bunch of kids are getting together to play street hockey."

"Elizabeth is still in charge. You know the rules," Chuck said. "You best be nice to your little brother and be home by nine. Not a second later. Got it?"

"Yes, sir," both boys said in unison.

"I'll keep an eye on them." Elizabeth waved.

"I got lucky when that girl's family moved in next door. Just glad I don't have a daughter. I'd be locking her up." Chuck pointed his finger toward the sliders. "I'm starting to get a little jealous over what Jett and my wife could possibly be talking about this long. He's quite the charmer."

"Well, I doubt it's limo rides and blow jobs," she said, needing some comic relief in the conversation.

"As if you told him that."

"He wouldn't drop it. You left me with no choice." She batted her eyelashes. "I mean, really, why the hell would you drop that bomb when you knew I was going up there to spend the night with him?"

"If I end up with another black eye before the night is over, I'm never speaking to you again."

"Promise, promises." Winslet laughed. But she had to admit, she was curious as to what Renee and Jett were so deep in conversation over while opening a second bottle of wine.

Or why it took so damn long.

## CHAPTER ELEVEN

"Let me get that." Jett took the wine bottle from Renee's hand.

"Thank you." Renee smiled. "So, how are you liking Fallport?"

"I love it here," Jett said as he stabbed the cork with the screw thing and twisted. While he loved a good glass of wine, he never understood this corkscrew thing. It made no sense to him, and it was a total pain in the ass. "I've only been here a week, but I couldn't be happier."

"You might go running out that door after this conversation." She handed him a decanter. "Seven days and you're already mixed up with someone I've known since grade school." She arched a brow. "I might not be Winslet's best friend, but I'm one of her longest friends, and we have some interesting, shared history."

He pounded his chest. "So I've heard."

"Oh, really. And which part are we referring to? Because whatever my idiot husband has said, I'm sure that's not what I'm talking about." She waved her hand before picking up a full glass of wine. "Chuck enjoys shocking the few men who openly date Winslet. He cares a great deal for her, and so do I. So, if he can throw them off-balance, which helps gauge what their intentions are or aren't, he'll bring up the fact they dated. Or mention one particular thing. It's ridiculous."

Jett wasn't sure if he was supposed to respond. And if he was, what the appropriate response should be. He respected and valued Chuck as a co-worker and a new friend.

His wife seemed lovely. A little rough around the edges, but so was Winslet.

He managed to wrangle the cork out of the wine bottle and poured it into the decanter.

"Cat got your tongue?" Renee asked.

He chuckled. "I'm usually quick-witted, but you're the one throwing me off-balance."

"I see." She leaned against the counter and smiled. "Well, I guess Chuck and his little hints at their past dating life didn't make you jealous or scare you off."

"Nope, but he only hinted. Winslet went into more detail than I ever needed to know."

"Good grief." Renee smacked her palm to her forehead. "But again, that's not what I was referring to and while I have the same sarcastic flair as my darling husband, I go about vetting people a little differently."

She lowered her chin. "While Winslet and I were close growing up, we had a short period of time where we wanted to throttle each other. Actually, we did get into a fistfight."

Jett chuckled. "Oddly, I think I might have enjoyed seeing that."

"Men. You're all the same." Renee shook her head. "I won't get into the sordid details as to why. It's old news, gossip, and frankly, shit she's not going to want me going on about."

He swallowed, wishing wine had been in his throat. Or maybe a good shot of whiskey. "Why do I get the feeling I'm about to be interrogated worse than I was with Chuck the last few days at work?" He cocked his head. "Because all he really did was harass me and told me I better not hurt her, or he'll come for the metal in my body with a chainsaw."

"So, you are really dating in the truest sense of the word." She folded her arms across her chest.

"I'm not sure Winslet would call it that, but I would." He honestly had no idea how Winslet would define what they were doing outside of having great sex. She had slept at his apartment for the last three nights and she would do so tonight. That was if he didn't put his foot in his mouth.

"To make a long story very short. Winslet and I went through something pretty traumatizing. It nearly destroyed our friendship." She pointed her finger toward the sliding glass doors. "If it weren't for my husband, I don't know if our friendship would have survived the drama. But it did and she was a bridesmaid at our wedding. We consider her to be family. For whatever reason, Chuck thinks you're the greatest thing since sliced bread."

"I kind of have a bro crush on him too." That wasn't a lie. He and Chuck had hit it off from day one.

"Tell me something I don't know." Renee laughed. "It's hard for both Chuck and me to watch Winslet aimlessly wander through her life acting as if she's happy with how it turned out. We know her and we know the kind of walls she's got built up. When she lets someone in, she lets them in so deeply they hold the power to crush her—"

"I'm sorry. I have to stop you." Jett understood Renee's concerns. If he were on the other side of this, he'd be doing exactly the same thing. "We've been seeing each other for a week. While I care about her, seven days isn't a very long time. That said, I have no intention of hurting her."

"If you had let me finish my statement, you'd understand that I'm less concerned about her, since her heart is already on the floor from something else I'm not going to get into with you, and I'm more worried about your feelings."

"Ah. I see." Jett ran his fingers through his hair. "First. I know all about what happened. And second, I'm a big boy. I absolutely know what I've gotten myself into."

"Are you sure about that?" Renee waggled her finger. "Not many men have loved Winslet. Off the top of my head, I can only think of one who actually truly, honestly loved her for exactly who she is."

"My knowledge of her past relationships is limited to your husband, Harvey, and the person to whom we will not speak of. So, I have no idea who you're talking about."

"This is going to sound weird coming from me, but Chuck is the only one who loved her for her. Now, he loves her like a sister. They've always had a unique bond. Harvey never understood. I think he was jealous of it."

"And what about you?"

Renee tossed her head back and laughed. Loud. "Good Lord, no. I was the third wheel all through their relationship. They just weren't meant to be and when they broke up, they were able to remain friends. I love that about those two. They wish nothing but love and happiness for each other. But you're missing my point."

"Which is?" Jett wasn't sure he wanted to hear this.

"Chuck tells me you're an incredibly logical man."

"He calls me Mr. Spock at work. I hate it."

"Well, I want you to process this, especially since you know what happened." She sipped her wine. "She didn't go into that last relationship thinking it would be forever. She hasn't done that since Harvey."

"She's not doing that with me." His heart thumped in his chest like a caged animal. "I'm not doing that."

"Maybe not. But you're both swimming in the deep end of the pool." She waggled her finger. "Without life jackets, I might add. For Winslet, that's a fight-or-flight place to be. You need to be prepared for that."

"I have a question for you," Jett said. "Why do you feel the need to tell me this?"

"Because I like you. My husband adores you. And because you're perfect for Winslet. But when she..."

The sound of the sliding glass doors opening interrupted Renee.

Jett turned his head.

"What on earth have you two been chatting about?" Chuck waved his hand, letting Winslet in. "We're dying of thirst out there."

Jett snagged the decanter and filled everyone's wineglasses. "Oh, we've been discussing how you have a man crush on me."

"I heard everyone at the ranger station is calling the two of you Jeuck." Renee bent over, placed her hands on her knees, and burst out laughing. "I should have made Jell-O for dessert. That way Winslet and I could watch you strapping men wrestle in your boxers."

"Babe, that's just gross." Chuck snagged a glass of wine and wrapped his arm around Renee. "That visual only works when it's two women."

"I will have to agree with Chuck on this one." Jett found himself smiling from ear to ear. "And that's partly because I've seen him in his boxers. Not something I want to see again."

"Oh, the things that are going on inside my head." Renee tapped her temple.

"You're weird." Chuck kissed his wife's cheek.

"Why is it strange for women to fantasize about two men?" Winslet leaned into Jett, and he looped his arm around her tiny waist. "But so totally normal for guys to get all hot and bothered about wanting to watch two girls go at it?"

"Seriously? We have to answer that question?" Jett asked.

"Yes," both women answered simultaneously.

"I thought the conversations I had with my sister were odd." Jett lifted his wine and took a nice long sip. "Especially when she started dating my best friend and coming to me for advice. Or condoms."

"I look forward to meeting you sister," Renee said.

"Come on. Let's take this back outside." Chuck opened the sliders. "You should have been around when we were all in high school. Or when we came home from college during the summers. We did some pretty crazy shit. But the best was when we'd sit around playing truth or dare."

"The only problem with that was all of us would almost always take the dare." Winslet laughed. "At one point, we have all streaked through the town."

"My sister's husband dared me to do that once. Only, I got caught." Jett eased into one of the chairs at the table. He hadn't had this much fun with a group of people in a long time.

Too long.

"I was sixteen and my mom had to come to County and pick me up. She read me the riot act at the station, but the second we got in the car, she turned her head, laughed, and told me how I wasn't as bright as my father because he never got caught." Jett looped his arm over the back of Winslet's chair and toyed with a few stray strands of hair.

"Did you ever do it again?" Winslet asked.

"I never got caught." He winked.

Jett's phone vibrated in his back pocket. He pulled it out, glanced at the screen, and mentally groaned.

"Are you going to answer?" Winslet leaned closer, glancing over his shoulder.

"Nope. I thought it might be my mom calling me back, but it wasn't." Jett didn't know why he felt the need to qualify all of that. Perhaps it was because he'd received a call from another woman. It didn't matter that it was his ex-girlfriend, and he'd already told Winslet she'd been reaching out.

He just didn't want to do it in front of their friends.

*Their friends.*

That should feel funny, but it didn't. And he did consider Chuck to be a close, personal friend.

However, he had no desire to deal with Becky. Not now. Maybe not ever. Granted, just a few short days ago, he was willing to entertain a phone call. Hell, he wasn't even sure he was over her.

But today?

She was his past.

Winslet was his present.

And he'd like her to be around more than a few months.

A thought that utterly terrified him. His chest tightened as if a boa constrictor had wrapped around his body. Evelynn had always accused him of falling in love hard and fast.

He couldn't deny it.

And he'd been in love three times, if he counted Piper, which he did.

It couldn't be happening again.

Winslet gently touched his wrist. "She's been calling and texting. Don't you think you should respond? Maybe something happened."

"We don't mind if you take a call," Chuck said. "You can step into the kitchen for some privacy."

Jett sucked in a deep breath. Becky was the last thing he wanted to deal with right now. He knew what she wanted. Evelynn had filled him in on that.

Before Winslet had turned his world upside down, he might have had some unresolved feelings about his past.

That was no longer the case.

In the last few days, he'd come to realize it wasn't that he'd been harboring a desire to have Becky in his life, but a need to reconcile what had happened. He'd done that by accepting he only served a single purpose in Becky's life.

He could no longer be that man.

For anyone.

Which stirred something else in his heart. He knew Winslet liked him. Even cared for him. And Winslet wasn't using him in the same vein as Becky. Or even Kiki. Jett wasn't Winslet's savior. Not in the same way because Winslet had a strong sense of who she was and what she wanted. Her main issue was a shift in her core fundamental goals in life—which had always been to have a family—but she shoved them deep in her soul to protect herself.

She could no longer do that, and Jett understood.

But if he was being honest with himself—he wasn't in that same space. Having a partner? He believed he could do that. But kids? He wasn't sure. He'd given up that concept when Kiki had left, and he hadn't thought too much about it since. His career had been his life.

But now he had more balance. His sister. His parents. They meant more. Well, they always did. But even those relationships had suffered because of his commitment to the military. He also had a better handle on what relaxation meant.

However, he wasn't sure all that added up to being a good father.

The real question was, why was he even thinking about it?

"You need to talk to her," Winslet said. "Clear the air. Not just for her, but for you. Too many things were left unsaid." She squeezed his hand. "I know it's hard, but I also know you want to put it in the past once and for all. If you don't, it's always going to haunt you." She lowered her chin. "Just like I'm going to have to face Shamus on Monday and have that hard conversation."

Damn woman had a point.

"Not to be a nosy bitch, but what and who are you talking about?" Renee asked, leaning forward and resting her elbows on the table. "You don't have to answer, but this is a safe space. We only gossip among ourselves."

Jett really loved Renee and Chuck's odd sense of humor. "To make a very long story short, my ex-girlfriend has been reaching out a lot lately. It comes on the heels of the government declassifying some information about the helicopter crash that nearly killed me and the rescue mission me and my team were on. It wasn't much information, but it does discuss her brother's death and how he was killed by the enemy hours before we were attacked. I was told a few months after the incident that we would have been too late. That my friend had already been dead before a single shot had been fired at me. But I couldn't tell that to Becky. I would have been court-martialed." Jett closed his eyes, taking a moment to collect his thoughts and rein in his grief.

So much carnage. So much pain. He could still hear the screams and smell the burning flesh of his friends. He remembered crawling on his belly, barely being able to breathe, much less use his legs, trying to get his buddies to safety while they took on heavy fire and more bullets ripped through his body before darkness overtook him.

He blinked.

Winslet inched closer. Her arm wrapped around his waist like a warm fleece. There was no look of disgust or even shock or pity on her beautiful face. Only kindness and caring.

And sadness.

Same with Renee and Chuck.

He wasn't used to this from anyone other than those he served with and his family.

Normally, war stories terrified people. They gasped. Or retreated at the horrors.

Or worse, tried to act as if they understood, when even he didn't—and he'd lived it.

"Becky is reliving Justin's death all over again. They were very close. The hard part is he was one of my closest friends. It's how Becky and I met. And she blamed me for him dying. That I somehow didn't do enough." The words tumbled out of his mouth so fast he couldn't stop. Winslet had heard it all before. But it felt good to say it again. To purge. To understand his dynamic with Becky.

With women in general.

"I remember when Zeke got the call about what happened to you. He bugged out of town so fast it made our heads spin," Chuck said. "He said they had to revive you, twice."

"That's what I'm told." Jett nodded. He tried to never focus on that. He was vertical. He was breathing. And he was damn fucking grateful. "The thing is, she's reaching out because I'm a connection to her brother. Not because she wants anything to do with me."

"Are you sure about that?" Renee asked.

"Yes," Jett said. "My sister had an interesting conversation with her, and it all comes back to my friendship with Justin. And the fact that she and I were a couple when he died."

"It goes deeper than that." Winslet pursed her lips. "You helped her through her darkest hour. She's looking for that same kind of comfort. While I believe she's toxic, I still think you should have a conversation with her." Winslet ran her hand up and down his back. "You cared about her once. Hell, you still care about her. But this chat would be about you, not her."

"Maybe. But it's not going to be tonight." He leaned in and kissed Winslet's cheek. "Time to change the subject."

"How about we talk about Cooper Wilks and the fact that he's been showing up at the police station every single day, bugging the shit out of Chief Hill and Weston. He's demanding an arrest." Chuck raised his glass, shaking his head. "Girl wonder over here hasn't even identified the bones yet."

"Not actually my job." Winslet laughed. "But we should know who she is by Monday, and I ran into Cooper yesterday. It was not pleasant."

"I saw him at the coffee shop this morning." Chuck ran his hand over his mouth. "He rambled on for twenty minutes about how he knew his wife hadn't run off with Marcus."

"Yeah, well, he doesn't believe my grandfather killed his wife either." Winslet twirled a piece of hair between her fingers. "He's had a few strange theories over the years, but it always comes back to my dad."

"Why does he believe your father killed his mother?" Jett asked. "I still don't understand that one."

"There were some inconsistencies in her dad's story," Renee said.

"The timeline is a little off." Winslet snagged her glass and took a gulp. "There was a report of gunshots being heard in the middle of the night. My father never heard them. The police found that to be suspect since he was asleep in the house. And then there was the dried blood on his clothing. People thought that was off. But he had no motive to kill his mother."

"I'm going to play devil's advocate here and ask a question that might get me in the doghouse, but did he know about the alleged affair? Or fight with his parents about something? And did they do a gun residue test?" Jett asked.

"To answer the first couple of questions, my dad admitted he'd heard a rumor, but it wasn't about Sarah and his father. It was about his mother and uncle. And Xavier is still kicking. Though, he's in a home and has dementia, so he wouldn't be much help today. As far as fighting goes, he never mentioned anything about that," Winslet said. "My father failed the residue test." She raised her hand. "But he'd been at the gun range the day before with my grandfather. There were eight witnesses to that. My father was ruled out ten hours after they brought him to the station and while rumors fly about that every once in a while, it's pretty much defunct."

"You're not starting to believe that her dad could have murdered her grandfather, are you?" Chuck cocked his head.

"It's not that, especially if there's no motive." Jett leaned back. "I spent a year between hospitals and rehabs. One of the things that got me through was watching true crime shows. Ever since then, my mind goes to weird places." He ran his fingers through his hair. "Weston asked me once if I wanted to peek through his files. I might do that. Maybe my weird, twisted mind can help."

"Not if you're going to go slinging your accusations at my dad." Winslet poked her finger at his shoulder. "He might be a cheating prick, but he's no murderer."

"I'm not looking to do that, just trying to help solve the case." Only, her father was an interesting angle.

Damn, he was an asshole.

# CHAPTER TWELVE

Jett blinked open his eyes, stretched, and rolled to his side. He reached for Winslet.

But she wasn't in bed.

He sat up, forcing his eyes to focus. The sound of the shower echoed in his ears. Reaching for his cell, he checked the time. Damn, he slept longer than he'd wanted to. He had less than an hour to get ready for work, especially if he planned on taking Winslet to the State lab.

But that was just enough time to join her in the shower.

He scowled.

Two missed calls and one text from Becky.

She would have to wait.

He had a girlfriend to satisfy.

The entire weekend had been filled with a lightness

he hadn't experienced in a long time. First, dinner with Chuck and Renee. That had been eye-opening. Then there was an afternoon with Tammy and her husband.

Interesting, to say the least.

And yesterday, a romantic mountaintop picnic. Deep down, he knew this was going way too fast. Every evening, he thought about suggesting that they not spend the night together, but he couldn't bring himself to do it. The idea of sleeping alone no longer seemed like an option.

And it should be.

This thing between them was casual.

She was leaving.

She'd made that perfectly clear a few times.

His sister was right. Her sister was right. Renee was right. Winslet was going to break his fucking heart and there was not a damn thing he could do about it. He wasn't even sure he could shrug his shoulders and be pragmatic anymore.

No thanks to Winslet.

When this was over, he was going to need a good grandma chat, because that was about the only way he'd be able to survive this one.

With his cell in his hand, he pulled back the covers and padded to the bathroom. As soon as he opened the door, he was assaulted with steam carrying the fresh scent of coconut. God, he loved that scent on a woman.

But not just any woman.

On Winslet.

He set the phone on the counter, pulled back the shower curtain, and stepped inside. "Good morning, beautiful." He wrapped his arms around her naked body, kissing her shoulder. "Did you sleep well?"

"I did." She leaned back, resting her head on his chest. "I was going to wake you as soon as I got out."

"This is so much better." He cupped her breast, fanning his thumb over her taut nipple. He couldn't get enough of her if he tried.

Her body responded to him instantly, goosebumps rising over her skin and a soft sigh escaping her lips. He relished every reaction, each a testament to their undeniable chemistry. His hands traveled downward, stroking the curve of her hips and tracing the soft lines of her body. There was an intoxicating allure to their morning entanglements that left Jett craving more.

Winslet turned in his arms, eyes sparkling amid the falling water droplets. "I'm glad you're here," she said, gingerly tracing his jawline with her fingers. A smile crept up on her face as she wrapped her arms around his neck, pulling him closer until their faces were mere inches apart.

He looked down at her, eyes filled with wonder and affection. This was dangerous territory he was treading but he found he couldn't tear his gaze away. He loved the way she looked at him—like he was the only thing in her world right now. And maybe he was. For this fleeting moment at least.

A husky laugh escaped his lips as he pressed his

forehead against hers. "I wouldn't be anywhere else," he murmured, brushing a loose strand of hair off her face and tucking it behind her ear.

Somewhere in the distance, his phone buzzed again, but they both chose to ignore it. Right now, there were no distractions, no obligations or responsibilities—just him and Winslet together in their small pocket of time where reality seemed to hold its breath.

And even though Jett knew that when this chapter closed he would be left with a gaping hole in his life, for now he chose to forget about tomorrow and lose himself in Winslet. One day at a time.

He let his hands wander lower, appreciating every reaction she gave him. Winslet bit her lip, her eyes never leaving his as she shivered under his touch. He reveled in the sound of her breathing, shallow and quickening under the steam and heat. Their bodies moved together in rhythm with the falling water, a dance as old as time itself yet uniquely their own.

A heavy sense of yearning washed over Jett. With each passing second, he was falling harder for Winslet—an undeniable fact that he couldn't ignore any longer. Ripples of fear coursed through him.

But he pushed them away, forcing his focus back to the woman in front of him. Winslet brought her hands up to cup his face, her touch soft and tender as she pulled him down for a kiss. It was deep and passionate, filled with an intensity that had his heart pounding in his chest. This was what he wanted—

every stolen moment, every stolen kiss, every stolen touch.

He could feel the tension building between them, a tangible entity that refused to be ignored any longer. Winslet's fingers tangled in his wet hair as she pulled him closer still. In response, he pressed himself against her, their bodies molding together perfectly. He could feel her heartbeat against his chest—strong, steady, and in sync with his own.

They were so deeply lost in each other that they neither heard nor cared about the outside world—his buzzing phone included. The water became colder, but that didn't seem to matter either. The heat between them was more than enough to compensate for it.

They lingered there, their passion spiraling out of control until finally they surrendered to their needs. The bathroom echoed with their soft moans and whispered promises of never-ending affection as they moved together in passionate rhythm.

Jett knew that Winslet held power over him unlike anyone else ever did. And while he did fear the impending heartbreak he was setting himself up for when she eventually left, he would never regret a single moment.

Wrapped in each other's arms, they spent a few more precious minutes under the lukewarm water before getting out of the shower. The tiny bathroom felt emptier without their shared warmth and laughter echoing around it.

Jett couldn't help but trace his fingers along Winslet's body one last time before bundling her into a fluffy towel. She smiled up at him, eyes sparkling with happiness and something that looked suspiciously like love.

But that couldn't be. It might be what he wished for, but it wasn't the truth.

"What is going on with your phone?" She turned, lifting the device off the counter. "Becky?" She glanced between his cell and him three times. "You haven't called her back?"

"Nope." He sighed.

"Aren't you the least bit curious as to what she has to say?"

"I think you're more interested than I am." He batted Winslet's nose. "And after speaking with my sister, we both know what she wants, and I can't be the person to give it to her. I not only don't feel that way for her anymore, but I also fear she needs the kind of help only a good therapist can give." Jett was a firm believer in honesty.

Sometimes that was considered a good thing.

Other times, not so much.

Winslet was a constant surprise.

Not once did she seem upset or jealous that his ex-girlfriend was chomping at the bit to get ahold of him.

"It's not that I feel the need to know why she's calling my boyfriend, but you need to change the dynamic. Not just for her, but for you."

He smiled. Wide. "Is that what I am?"

"Would you have preferred me call you my flavor of the month? Or the guy I'm screwing?"

"Absolutely not." He scowled.

"Okay, then." She waved his phone in front of his face, which inadvertently unlocked it. "Call her back. Now. And put it on speaker."

He narrowed his eyes.

"Do it. Or I will." She palmed his cheek. "I'll step out if you want me to, but I'd rather not."

"My gosh. Is Winslet Payne jealous?"

"I'm getting there." She lifted her finger. "And you do have a bleeding heart when it comes to a damsel in distress."

He chuckled. "Fine." He took his cell and pressed the return call button. It rang only once.

"Jett. Hi. I thought you'd never call me back," Becky's voice screeched across his ears like a singer out of tune.

It made him sad because at one time, he liked the sound of her voice. But it also told him he had let go of the past and moved on.

That was a good thing.

"I'm sorry, but I've been busy," he said. "Your message and texts said you needed to talk to me. About what?"

"Oh. Um. Well. I heard you moved. I was kind of surprised by that."

He let out a long sigh. "I did."

"Your sister didn't tell me where."

He sucked in a deep breath and let it out slowly. He could hear the pain in Becky's voice. He didn't want to add to that. He didn't want to hurt her, but she needed to move on. She needed to grieve her brother. And Jett couldn't help her. "Virginia."

"I'm sure your family misses you," Becky said. "I miss you."

Winslet folded her arms across her chest.

He pinched the bridge of his nose. This was not what he needed. The only thing he wanted from Becky was an apology for the shitty things she'd said.

But he no longer cared about that.

However, he did care about her well-being.

"I'm sorry, Becky, but it's a little too late for us to be having this conversation."

"I know I said some things, but you have to understand. I'd just lost my brother. I was grappling with grief and with so few answers. You couldn't even give me that and you knew all along he'd been killed before... before..."

"Everything about my mission was classified. Most of it still is. I know that's always been really hard for you." He ran his hand across the scar on his chest, feeling his heart pump blood through his veins. "I miss Justin too. He was a good man. But Becky, you need to talk to someone. Someone who isn't me. A professional. I know the information the government gave you was difficult to digest, but I can't be the person you lean on."

Winslet pushed his hand aside and pressed her lips against the center of his chest. She wrapped her loving arms around his body.

God, she felt so good. So warm. It was as if she understood the torment that ripped through his soul.

He didn't want to hurt Becky. He could forgive her for everything she said. For walking out on him. That was easy. But he couldn't even entertain being her friend. Not now. Probably never.

"Why did they wait so long to release that? To tell the families?"

"Look, Becky. I spent most of my life in the military and I don't even have an answer for that. But like I said, I can't be the person you turn to. I do understand you're hurting. I get that. I wish you nothing but happiness and I would be grateful if you could find that. I really would. But I've moved on. It took a long time for me to get there. However, I'm finally living my life again."

"What does that mean?" she asked with an indignant tone. The same one she always used when she got pissed off about something. Or when a conversation switched from her to someone else. Or when she wasn't getting what she thought she needed. It's what made their relationship difficult and why it had been so easy for him to let her walk out that door.

"It just means I moved past survival mode. I've got a

job and I'm happy," he said. "Find a good therapist. You can work through this."

"It's hard sometimes, you know?"

"I do," he said. "But you're strong. You'll get through it, and you know your brother would want you to be happy. He wouldn't want you to be holding on to all this anger and pain over him. He died doing what he loved."

"I was happy with you." She sniffled.

Jett let out a long breath. "Becky, we can't do this. I can't do this. I'm sorry."

"I could come to Virginia. We could have dinner or something," Becky said softly. "It's just... just... I don't know. I feel like we never really had closure."

"No. We're past that." He rested his chin on top of Winslet's head. "This might sound harsh, and maybe it is. But I found closure. It took time, but you made it quite clear when you walked out of my hospital room. I accept that. I need you to do the same now."

"I just thought maybe we could talk. Get to know each other again."

"I can't. I'm seeing someone. Someone I care about very much."

Winslet tilted her head and arched a brow.

"Oh. I see," Becky said. "Your sister didn't tell me that."

"Take care of yourself, Becky."

"I hope she's not a Kiki. Don't call me if she breaks your heart." The line went dead.

"I'm sorry. While she sounds really sad and I feel bad for her, what she said at the end wasn't fair. Not to mention she's only appealing to your strong sense of honor, duty, and your own emotions over what happened."

"I'm well aware." He struggled with his desire to leave the past where it belonged and wanting to help Becky move forward in her life. But he knew he'd never be the one who could do that. She hadn't loved him. Not really. Even if he had left the military, they had other issues in their relationship, a fact he had to face. "What you didn't see on my phone was a text I got from my sister late last night. She warned me that Becky wasn't doing well at all. That she's still struggling with her brother's death and in a constant state of depression. I'm not the only man from her past she's reached out to." He pulled Winslet close. "I don't know what I would do if something ever happened to Evelynn. She's a total pain in the ass sometimes, but she's also my best friend."

"I know you still care about Becky," Winslet whispered. "I don't fault you for that. But you can't be responsible for her."

"I loved her once," he admitted. "I really do hope she finds the help she needs." He cupped Winslet's chin. "I'm glad I got to talk to her, but I do worry I might have done more damage than good."

"I doubt that. You were honest and kind. The rest is up to her." Winslet smiled. "You're a good man." She kissed him on the cheek before stepping out of the bathroom. Jett watched her leave, his heart filled with a bittersweet ache.

He knew he was in deep. There was no denying it anymore.

She was going to break his heart.

And he wouldn't have it any other way.

# CHAPTER THIRTEEN

Winslet should have taken her own vehicle to the State lab. She was playing a foolish game, and there was no guarantee Shamus would even see Jett drop her off.

Or pick her up.

What difference did it make anyway?

She didn't want Shamus in her life, so there was no worry of her succumbing to his charm. Not that he would turn it up. He'd made it very clear that he was in love with his wife.

This week would prove to be quite difficult. Shamus was only one of the reasons. Work was another one, especially if the bones proved to be Hannah Wilks. But the one that was the heaviest on her mind was the conversation she would be having with Emory. She owed it to her best friend to take this career opportunity seriously. Becoming head of the department would be a big deal. It would be the first time she had a steady position.

Ever.

It would give her the maximum opportunity to work with both state and federal crime units, and she loved that idea.

But then there was Jett.

This thing with him happened so fast and furious she couldn't untangle her heart from her mind. She needed a moment to think. To separate her emotions and do what Jett did best.

Be logical.

Something she normally prided herself on. But every time she thought about this damn job, there were only two things she could think about.

Jett.

And her father.

Those were strictly emotional reasons for either leaving. Or staying.

"You've been awfully quiet this entire ride." Jett reached across the cab of his truck and took her hand. "Are you okay?"

"Yeah," she said.

"You're not very convincing."

"I'm worried about who those bones belong to." She turned her head as they pulled into the parking lot.

"And seeing Shamus?" Jett rolled his truck to a stop in front of the main doors.

"He's the least of my concerns," she admitted. "I'll be

more worried when his wife and kids show up. But I'm in a much better headspace about all that thanks to my little sister." Winslet laughed. "I'm really enjoying how our friendship is growing. She's quite the little firecracker."

"That she is." He shifted in his seat. "Something else is bugging you. Talk to me."

"It's not a conversation we should have before I head into work." It was strange how easy it was to be honest with Jett. Or how much she didn't want to lie to him, which she wondered if she should. She glanced at the clock on the dash. Not that she punched a time clock with the state police.

He arched a single brow. "I'm not leaving now until you at least hint at what's got you furrowing your forehead."

She let out a long sigh. "I'm seriously considering taking a full-time position at the university."

"Really." His lips curved into a smile. It wasn't a big one. As a matter of fact, it was as though he was trying not to smile.

All that did was bring one to her mouth.

"Oh my God. Don't let that go to your head." She playfully slapped his shoulder. "There is still a big part of me that sure as shit doesn't want to stay in this town. I can't deal with my father. And he's being all weird about me and Tammy being close."

"Yeah. You showed me that text. It was strange. Who wouldn't want their children to have a decent relationship. It was like he wanted a wedge between you and then to ask about the bones. That seemed odd as well."

"Everyone in town is curious about that," she said. "For whatever reason, he's threatened by me being close with Tammy."

Jett chuckled. "My mom gets jealous sometimes over how tight Evelynn and I are."

"Tammy said my dad has been acting off all week. I think he's paranoid. Maybe my mom's finally smartening up. Wouldn't that be nice."

Jett reached out and traced her jawline. "You're changing the subject again."

"I know. And it's because I don't know what I'm going to do." She pressed her hand over his mouth. "While I do care about you and I'm enjoying what's happening between us, you can't be the reason I stay. I have a lot to consider. My career. My life goals. My family. My team. It's a lot."

He curled his fingers around her wrist and kissed her palm. "As long as I'm not the reason you leave."

"That wouldn't be the case, but I'm trying not to factor you into my decision. I'm sorry if that hurts you."

"Please, Winslet. We've been dating for a week." He leaned in and brushed his lips across hers in a tender, loving kiss. "I'd be lying if I said I didn't want you to stay. But I'm not going to pressure you. This is your career. Something you've worked on your whole adult life. It matters to you. Therefore, it matters to me."

"You're not helping." She palmed his now full beard. "I really like this on you."

"I could never keep it when I was in the military. Ultimately, I'm lazy, so it's nice not to have to shave every day," he said. "After work, why don't we sit down and chat about your job offer. You know how pragmatic I can be. I promise I won't toss myself into a reason to stay."

"I honestly believe that about you."

"Come on. I'll walk you to the door."

She lowered her chin and arched a brow.

All he did was laugh and open the truck door. Deep down, she knew if she took the job, he would be one of the reasons she did.

Putting her heart on the line sometimes sucked.

But before she did that, she needed to know a few things and that would be a difficult conversation. A conversation that was way too soon. However, she needed to have it if she was going to stay.

She took his hand and slipped from the passenger seat. Tossing her backpack over her shoulder, she strolled toward the main doors.

"Jett? Jett McCoy, is that you?" a female voice rang out from somewhere behind her.

She glanced over her shoulder and her heart plummeted to her toes. Her tongue stuck to the roof of her mouth as if it were laced with superglue.

There stood Shamus and his wife.

"Holy shit. Feya Thompson. I can't believe it. What the hell are you doing in Fallport, Virginia?" Jett's arm circled around her waist as he pulled her tight. He knew what Shamus looked like, so he had to know he was staring at the man. It didn't take a genius to make the connection.

"It's Feya Quinn now." She smiled sweetly. The woman was gorgeous with her long blond hair, stunning blue eyes, and tiny little figure. She pressed her hand on Shamus' chest, her wedding ring sparkling in the sun. "This is my husband Shamus." She glanced up at him with adoring eyes. "Shamus, Jett and I went to high school together. Well, he was a couple of years older. I actually graduated with his sister." She turned her head. "How is Evelynn? Gosh. I haven't seen or talked to her since our five-year reunion. I did hear she married Doug. That had to have been weird for you."

"Not at all. They have two kids now." Jett pressed his lips on Winslet's temple. "This is my girlfriend, Winslet."

Feya's pretty smile disappeared, and her eyes grew wide with what appeared to be shock. She pursed her lips and then cleared her throat. "Oh. Are you the same Winslet that was on the dig in Africa with my husband?"

"She is," Shamus said. "Hey, Winslet. It's good to see you again. I was told you would be working on this case and that I would be speaking to your students."

"That you are." Winslet nodded. Damn, this had to be the most awkward thing she'd ever done. "And it's nice to see you too." But it wasn't.

"Sweetie, you didn't mention someone you've worked with before would be here," Feya said.

"Babe, I honestly didn't think about it." Shamus looped his arm around his wife. "I need to get going. I'm behind on this case and I need to read up." He kissed his wife. "I'll see you in there, Winslet." He nodded. "It was nice meeting you, Jett."

"See you around." Jett squeezed her hip so hard, she worried he might have left fingerprints. It didn't hurt, but she could tell it was taking all Jett's energy not to say something crazy.

She appreciated Jett for being kind.

But what a strange turn of events this was.

"So, Jett. Last I heard, you were in the Army. What happened?"

"It was time to leave," he said. "I'm now a park ranger and if I don't get going, I'm going to be late for work."

"Well, it was good seeing you again. And nice to meet you, Winslet." Feya turned on her heel and headed toward a nice shiny rental.

Jett wrapped his arms around Winslet, resting his chin on top of her head.

She buried her face in his chest and sighed. "I can't believe you know his wife."

"She was a friend of Evelynn's. She used to sleep

over at my house. They lost touch right around the time Feya got married. I remember that distinctly because Evelynn kind of felt like Feya dropped her entire friend group for her new husband. But Feya did move away, and I guess was constantly moving a lot."

"Nature of the beast when you do what Shamus and I do, unless you take a professorship."

Jett cupped her face. "Not to make this any harder than it already is, but Feya was always a nice girl. A little clingy and needy. But I always thought she was sweet."

"Please tell me you didn't date her."

"I did not." He kissed her nose. "I'm working in the office this morning, and then I'll be up at the second post, which has cell reception. Text or call if you need me. I mean it. If I'm not tending to something, I'll answer."

"You might regret that offer."

"I can't regret anything with you." He kissed her good and hard. It was the kind of kiss that didn't belong in public. But she didn't care. Whether this lasted only another day, a week, a month, or forever, she'd cherish every second she had with Jett.

Even his logicalness could be endearing.

Because the man had a heart of fucking gold.

WINSLET PUSHED OPEN the door to the lab and was greeted by a scowling Shamus. She glanced around, but no one had come in yet. Gently, she closed the door.

This would not be pleasant.

"What the fuck, Winslet? Seriously? Your boyfriend went to school with my wife? How did you manage that one? Or did you put out an ad for anyone who—"

"Shut up." She dropped her bag on the desk in the corner and snagged her white lab coat. "Jett and I were just as surprised as you were by that revelation and honestly, I'd rather not talk about the fucked-up situation *you* put us all in. I need you to focus on the soil, possible insects that were on the bones, and all your expertise so we can find out where this body might have been buried before she was found on that trail."

"I will dive into my job in a second, but I need to know that you and what's his name will stay clear of—"

"Oh my God, Shamus. I have no desire to blow up your life. If that were the case, I would have done it months ago. But since you brought it up, she deserves so much better than you. Honestly, you're a two-timing prick. If you didn't have small children, I would be telling her and not because I want to hurt you, but because she should know the truth and be able to decide for herself what she wants. Only, you know all this about me because I told you about my dad." She waved her finger under his nose. "For as long as you are here, don't bring it up again. Let's do our jobs and stay out of each other's way."

Before Shamus could respond to her little rant, Emory came strolling through the door. She paused at the threshold and groaned. Loudly. She scrunched her face, and it looked like she ate something that tasted worse than three-day-old fish. "Hello, Shamus. I can't say I'm glad to see you again."

"This is going to be a fun couple of weeks," Shamus said under his breath. He stood in front of a few samples, lifted a clipboard, and stared at… Winslet had no idea, and she didn't care.

She hugged Emory. "How was your weekend?"

"Splendid. Yours?"

"Amazing. Jett is dying for the four of us to get together. We'll have to do that this weekend now that Oliver is back for a bit."

"Are we still on for Wednesday night?" Emory bit down on her lower lip.

Emory had fallen in love with Fallport. With the university. She and Oliver had never made demands. They had been as loyal as they came, and Winslet owed it to them—to herself—to honestly look at this offer.

She was pushing forty.

It was time to stop moving from one guest spot to the next. From one crazy dig site to the next.

It wasn't just Emory and Oliver that needed stability for their family. Winslet needed it too. She craved it. And fucking bloody hell, she wanted it with Jett of all people.

How the hell did someone fall in love so quickly? And could she really trust that emotion?

"Absolutely. I'm looking forward to the conversation," Winslet said.

"Are you really?"

"Yes, Emory." She smiled. "I haven't made any decisions, but I want to muddle through all the details. I'm honestly open to the idea."

"Or maybe you're just open to Jett."

"He is adorable, isn't he."

Shamus coughed.

Winslet had totally forgotten he was in the room. A weight had been lifted off her shoulders. Her heart had a new lightness about it. It beat a little faster and with purpose. Being with Jett was a risk. But he didn't feel like a complication. It wasn't hard being with him, not like it had been with Shamus.

Jett was open. Honest. Perhaps to a fault. He shared things about his life. His family. She'd even had a conversation with his sister, which should have been awkward, but it wasn't. Jett took life on as it happened, something she wished she was better at. Sure, he was a wounded man. Both literally and figuratively.

But he was a man who was constantly grateful to be alive and maybe share a little bit of that with someone else.

She just wished he wanted a family.

The fact he'd made it clear fatherhood wasn't for him took all the wind out of her sails and it could be the deciding factor in everything. It shouldn't be. She barely knew the man. A little over a week didn't make for a great romance. But there was something about Jett that made her insides turn to mush.

Damn, how her life had changed.

"He certainly is." Emory nodded like a bobblehead. "I saw him in the parking lot as I was coming in. He's so kind. Always has something nice to say. I'm so glad you met him."

"Ladies, we have work to do," Shamus interjected.

Emory rolled her eyes.

The door to the lab swung open and Weston strolled in decked out in his police uniform. "Good morning," he said.

"Weston. What brings you by?" Winslet asked.

He glanced in Shamus' direction and narrowed his stare while he looped his fingers in his belt. "I have news." He jerked his chin. "And who is this?"

"Our colleague. Shamus Quinn."

"Nice to meet you." Weston widened his stance and turned his attention back to Winslet, catching her gaze. "We have identified the body and before it's made public, I wanted to let you know."

"Well, shit. It's Hannah Wilks." Winslet leaned against the counter, ignoring Weston's look of disgust over being in the same room with Shamus.

Weston wasn't an overly judgmental man, but when someone hurt a friend, the gloves came off. While his facial expressions didn't give too much away, his seething stare did. It tore through her body like a rocket. It wasn't directed at her, but she figured he had no desire to engage in any small talk with a lying cheat like Shamus.

Who would?

"According to the dental records from what you gave us, I'm afraid so." Weston nodded. "I'm headed over to Cooper's place after I leave here."

"That's not going to go well," Winslet said.

"Nope." Weston reached out and squeezed her forearm. "Can we go out in the hall for a second?"

"Sure." She followed Weston through the door. "What's going on?"

"I didn't want to say this in front of that asshole and wasn't sure if you wanted Emory or anyone else hearing this," Weston said. "But Chief Hill wants me to bring in your dad for questioning."

"I guess I shouldn't be surprised." She blinked as that statement hit her brain like a wild bull. "But why would he have killed his parents?"

"I don't have an answer for that. You know there are holes in the original story he gave the police. Things don't add up. And there are things in that file that were never released to the public. Not even you."

She cocked her head. "You've been holding out on me all these years. I can't believe this."

"It's standard police procedure. You know that." Weston sucked in a deep breath and let it out in a puff. "Haven and I would have told you, and honestly, we don't know what to make of the two pieces of information that don't make sense."

"Can you tell me now?"

"I'm going to, but you have to promise me that it stays between us."

"Can I discuss it with Jett?" Jesus. Where the fuck did that come from? Okay. Jett did have a unique brain. And his ability to strip emotion out of everything would be helpful.

Not to mention he was technically her boyfriend.

And not a fake one at this point either.

"I'll grant you that," Weston said. "As you know, gunshots were reported in the middle of the night that your father states he slept through. The neighbors, whom we can't question again because one is deceased and the other is in the same boat as your uncle, told the police they believed it came from inside your grandparents' home."

"That's a given."

Weston nodded. "But the same neighbors also told us they saw Cooper Wilks' pickup early that morning in your grandfather's driveway. They said they were going to get the paper."

"What was Cooper doing there?"

"Thing was, they told the cops that it wasn't Cooper, but Hannah."

"All this does is perpetuate the concept that my grandfather killed his wife and ran off with Hannah."

"Then we have to ask ourselves, why did he kill

Hannah?" Weston held up his hand. "But this is why the cops never released that information. Cooper's truck was never reported missing because it was back in his driveway before he even got out of bed."

"Cooper never had an alibi for any of this."

"He was never really a suspect, and he passed the residue test." Weston arched a brow. "There's one more thing."

"What's that?"

"The reason your father was questioned so hard was because the police found a pair of bloody sneakers by the back door. They belonged to your dad. His statement was that he found his mother. Dropped to his knees. Got blood all over him. Tried to see if she was alive and then raced out the door. He was barefoot and wearing pajama bottoms and a T-shirt."

"I know about the sneakers. He said he tripped over them."

Weston nodded. "That's the story. But to be honest, those sneakers look as though someone stepped through blood while wearing them."

"Are you saying my father's a suspect in both his mother and Hannah's murders?"

"He's officially a person of interest," Weston said. "But we also still have a missing man. What happened to your grandfather? Because you already told me that the woman who was found on that trail was in her thirties. Hannah was thirty-four when she went missing. She could have been murdered that morning. So could have your grandfather."

"Or he could have killed both his wife and… yeah. That doesn't make sense. Why would he kill both wife and lover?" She grabbed a wad of hair and twisted it, letting her forensic mind take over, shoving aside the fact that this was her family. Her father. "But why would my dad kill all of them? What's his motive? And he was fucking fourteen years old."

"That's a tough one. If your grandpa was having an affair with Hannah, I get murdering those two, but not your grandma."

"Unless she somehow wound up as collateral damage."

"Or maybe it was Hannah? Maybe she stumbled in on something that morning when she showed up? Hannah and your grandma were close."

"Yeah, but when was she seen at my grandparents' house?"

"Five in the morning," Weston said.

"What would she be doing there that early?"

"I don't know, but I will be asking Cooper that question."

"Jesus, this is a clusterfuck." She folded her arms across her chest. Her dad was many things. A liar. A cheat. He could be distant and cold sometimes, but throughout her childhood, she remembered him as being a good dad. A present father.

He couldn't be a murderer.

She shivered.

"When are you bringing in my dad?" she asked.

"Haven's heading there now, but please don't go warning him. Or anyone else in your family. I didn't have to tell you any of this." Weston lowered his chin and gave her his best cop look. It was menacing, but it made her chuckle.

"I won't. You have a job to do, and I want answers. I want the truth, but please, keep me in the loop."

"I'll call you later." He squeezed her arm.

She patted her back pocket. Shit, her phone was in her bag in the lab. She needed—wanted—to text Jett. She needed someone who would understand and be there without judgment. Someone who wouldn't coddle her. Or tell her stupid things, like everything was going to be okay. Or that he was sure her father hadn't done it. Or the cops had it all wrong.

She wasn't stupid.

She could see the reality.

She wanted to believe her father was innocent, and he probably was.

But this was damning.

# CHAPTER FOURTEEN

The last thing Jett wanted to do was spend his lunch break with anyone other than Winslet. Or maybe Chuck.

But he definitely didn't want to be sitting across a picnic table from Feya.

Especially when she looked like she'd been crying.

Worse when Chuck was glaring from the porch of the main office.

"What's going on?" he asked in the kindest of tones he could muster, doing his best to hide his frustration.

"I'm real sorry to bother you at work, but when I called, your co-worker mentioned when you'd be on break and I… I…" She swiped at her cheeks. "…well, I needed to ask you something personal."

"All right." He raised his soda and took a massive gulp. He never did drama well. He avoided it like the plague. Growing up, his sister had a few friends who were always causing trouble. Feya wasn't one of them, but she did bring with her a fair share of histrionics. She wasn't part of the mean girl crowd, but her desire to be popular drove Evelynn nuts.

It wasn't Evelynn's thing. She couldn't have cared less about who liked her and who didn't. She cared more about what kind of a person someone was than anything else. It's kind of how they were raised. Actions spoke louder than words.

"I'm real sorry to drop this at your feet," Feya said. "About six years ago, my husband had an affair."

Oh fuck. This was not the conversation he wanted to have with anyone. But especially not her. This was not his business, and he'd made a promise to Winslet.

But now he was smack-dab in the middle of a raging river without a life vest and no ability to swim to shore.

"I'm sorry," he managed.

"It sucked. I had just had our second child." She pulled out a tissue and dabbed her eyes. "Our kids are with his parents right now."

As if he needed to know that.

"Anyway. I love Shamus. So, we went to counseling, and I forgave him. He promised me no more digs. That he'd look for a professorship. But his field is so competitive, and we moved like every year, going from one guest lecture to the next."

Jett took another long slow sip of his beverage. He'd

always been a good listener. But this was going to take a lot of energy.

"He was on track for the position he has now, but then a dig came up in Africa and he really wanted to go. He said it would be the last one. It was only three months, and then he had this one semester before he was sure he'd get a professorship. Which he did." She sniffled. "Deep down I knew he was cheating on me again. I saw the signs. I chose to ignore them. We had kids. A beautiful life together. And then a few months ago, I knew he must have ended it because things went back to the way they were before. Maybe I'm a fool to believe that he'll never do it again because he's now in a permanent position. I don't know. It's just that I never thought I'd have to come face-to-face with the woman he was cheating on me with."

Jett sucked in a deep breath and let it out slowly. "What are you talking about?"

"Your girlfriend. I thought you should know, just in case there was some crossover or something. I feel like a jerk for telling you. No one told me. I'm sure people knew. Know. Some of our friends look at me with pity in their eyes. But I love my family. I love Shamus. I don't want to fail at this."

For the first time in a long while, Jett had no idea what to say or what to do. He couldn't break Winslet's trust. She meant too much to him to do that. But Feya was obviously in a lot of pain.

He glanced over his shoulder. Chuck leaned against

the post near the office. "Feya, I'm sorry, but will you excuse me for a moment? I need to check in with that man over there. It will just take a minute."

"Um, yeah. Sure."

Jett rose and strolled across the pathway. He jogged up the five steps and pulled out his cell.

"Enjoying your little date?" Chuck asked with a little bit of venom to his words.

"For the record, that's Shamus' wife. Talk about a small world, I went to high school with her," Jett said. "Follow me in the office for a second."

"Okay."

With his heart rattling in his chest, Jett tapped Winslet's contact information. "Come on, pick up the phone, babe."

"Hey, this is a nice surprise," Winslet's voice boomed over the airwaves.

"You're not going to think that when I tell you who showed up to have lunch with me or what she just informed me of, and I literally don't have a fucking clue as to what to do. I left her at the picnic table after she dropped the bomb because I don't know what to say. Oh, and Chuck is with me. You're on speaker."

"Oh my. You've got your panties in a twist," Winslet said. "I've never heard you shaken before. It's cute."

"Actually, it's not, Winslet." Chuck peered out the window. "Shamus' wife is here."

"Fuck me," Winslet muttered.

"Yup. And she knows he had an affair. And she

knows it was with you. She came here to warn me because no one told her. What do you want me to do? Babe, this is your call. It's your story to tell."

"She's really rattled you," Winslet said. "I'm truly sorry you're now in the middle of it but tell her the truth. Especially if she already knows. I just don't care anymore."

"Are you sure you want me to do that? I mean, she's a mess. I don't think knowing he lied to you will help matters. It might just crush her more."

"Shamus is being such a dick here at work. He doesn't care about anything other than getting caught. He's made that quite clear. Honestly, if she can pull herself together after the fallout, she'll be better off without him."

"I agree with Winslet," Chuck said. "I've lived in this town my whole life except for college. And I'm sorry to say this, but Winslet's mother is miserable. That poor lady out there, she'll just become a shell of a woman if she continues to stay with a man who keeps cheating."

"Yeah, she did mention he did it six years ago," Jett mumbled. "Okay. Wish me luck."

"I'll see you after work." The line went dead.

"You going to be okay?" Chuck slapped his back. "Do you need a wingman?"

"No. But Feya out there might need another decent human to lend an ear and maybe a shoulder to cry on."

"Why do some men have to be such assholes?"

"I have no idea, but someone better keep an eye on

me. I might seem like a levelheaded guy, but I won't be able to keep my fists to myself if I have to be in the same room with that man again."

WINSLET ENDED up catching a ride home with Emory since her work at the lab had been completed early. There was nothing left to do with the bones. Thank God.

Shamus determined that the bones had been buried somewhere in Virginia, most likely in or around Fallport.

Weston hadn't called.

But both her sister and her mother had been flipping out over her dad being hauled to the police station. Her mom had been furious. She ranted for over a half hour about what a weasel Weston was and how dare he feel the need to ask questions anywhere but the comforts of home.

Tammy had a different take.

She actually wondered if their father could have done it. That had been an interesting conversation.

She took the glass of wine Jett offered and snuggled into the sofa. "So, how was your day?"

"Fucking peachy." He set his glass on the table, pulled his shirt over his head, and flopped on the sofa, lifting his legs and setting his bare feet on the ottoman. "I've never seen so many tears come from one woman in my whole life. Even Chuck was at a loss."

"I wonder what she's going to do."

"I have no idea," Jett said. "When she finally stopped crying—which was weird because it was like she turned a valve and the waterworks ended—she stood, smoothed down her pants, thanked us for being honest, and left."

"You have a history with her, so you have to have some insight."

"I called my sister and asked her what she thought, and Evelynn said Feya would do one of three things. Quietly pack her bags and leave. Or try to talk him into counseling and work things out." He leaned forward, lifted his wineglass, and chugged half of it. "Or go ballistic."

"What does that look like?"

"I don't have a clue, but whatever it is, it doesn't sound good. But it's not our problem either."

"I'm sorry you were put in that position."

He turned and lifted her chin with his palm. God, he could be so tender. "You didn't. Shamus did."

"I don't know how you can say that. You're not the one who dated him."

"Nope. But he's the one who lied. To both of you." He kissed her, soft and tender. "Now, you said there was something you wanted to talk to me about before we dived into the whole *should I take this professorship* job."

"It's actually the head of the department now, but that's splitting hairs."

"And you're changing the subject."

She twirled her hair with her free hand. "This is going to be weird and awkward."

"Nothing could be stranger than today."

"The truth is I want to take the job. What's stopping me more than anything is I'm honestly worried about the possibility of my father being arrested."

"You really think he could have done it?"

"The things Weston told me, it's possible. What we're lacking is motive. But let's say the worst thing happens. I have to live in a town where my father is now a cheat and a murderer."

"You're being quite logical about this."

"My boyfriend taught me how." She laughed. "Haven lived through a ton of shit when she came back. And she survived."

"I know her story and that had to have sucked for her."

"It did. But she held her head high and now she's a freaking cop with an awesome husband and two kids. If she can do it, considering what she went through, so can I."

Jett traced his finger across her jawline. "You're a strong woman and the reality is no one can blame you for someone else's sins."

"You say that, but people do."

"True. But people do get past it," he said. "So, if it's

not your family's history or your dad stopping you from taking the job, what is?"

"This thing with us happened out of the blue. And it's happening so fast. I know I said I wouldn't factor you into my decision and maybe I won't. But I need to know a few things."

"I think you know me well enough to know you can ask me anything and I'll be honest."

That's what she was afraid of. "Do you have any desire to move back to Western, New York? You're so close with your family."

"I love my parents. And you've heard me and my sister talk. I don't know what I would have done without them after the helicopter crash. But I have lived my entire adult life away from them. I don't have to live next to them to be close. And sometimes, they can be stifling. Overbearing and bit much. So, the answer to the question is no. Next."

She chuckled before taking another sip of courage. "Would you ever get married again?"

Both brows shot up.

Shit. Too soon. Too fast.

"I'm not talking about us, per se," she added.

"But you are." He leaned in and kissed her cheek. "As way in the future. And it's a reasonable question considering you are making a change in your life, and we are a couple."

"We've known each other going on two weeks. That doesn't make for—"

He hushed her with his index finger. "I've honestly never been opposed to marriage. Only, after Kiki, I was soured to the concept. When Becky came into my life, I was thinking about it again. But you know what happened there. I believe in love. I believe in having a partner. I never thought I would be in a position to do it again. And yet I find myself sitting on this couch with you, biting my tongue, because I might consider begging you to stay."

"That's kind of sweet but dances around the answer."

"If all the stars aligned, yeah, I'd do it again."

Her heart damn near jumped out of her mouth and landed in his lap.

"Any more questions for me?"

"One," she whispered. "What about children?"

He downed the rest of his wine. "I can't believe I'm going to say this because after Kiki walked out on our marriage, I swore I'd never entertain that thought. I certainly didn't think about it with Becky." He set his glass down while she held her breath. Palming her face, he stared into her eyes as if he were looking into her soul. "When I was younger, all I wanted was a family. I used to dream of having a couple of kids to bounce on my knees. Part of that dream died when Kiki divorced me. I think part of me thought I wouldn't be a good dad because I wasn't a good husband."

"Stop that. I might have only been dating you a ridiculously short period of time, but all you've ever done is show me kindness. Okay, so maybe you could show a little more emotion sometimes, but you do when it counts."

He dropped his forehead to hers. "You've brought me full circle. You've made me think about things I haven't in years. It's crazy. Insane, even. I've never felt so alive before, and trust me, the moment they took me off a ventilator and I took my first breaths on my own, that felt like I was fucking alive."

"I can only imagine."

"My point is, I can't promise you anything. Actually, I won't promise something that I can't guarantee. But all these things that you're asking me are things I've thought about. But I wasn't going to bring them up because I didn't want to pressure you. I didn't want to make this about me. It's your career. Your life. I will support you no matter what because I—"

*Knock. Knock. Knock. Knock.*

"Whoever that is has horrible timing." He kissed her forehead and jumped to his feet while the pounding on his door continued. "Jesus. I'm coming." He gripped the door handle and pulled it back.

"You motherfucking asshole."

Winslet knew that voice.

She leaped to her feet.

The sound of knuckles connecting with Jett's cheek rattled her teeth.

Jett stumbled backward, slamming into her body. He twisted, but there was nothing he could do to prevent them both from falling to the floor with a thud.

"You think you're a big man? You think just because you knew my wife a long time ago you had the right?" Shamus towered over Jett. His eyes were filled with rage.

Winslet gasped. Fear filled her belly like sour milk. She'd never seen him so angry and out of control.

"And you." He stuck his finger in her face. "So much for not being a vindictive bitch." He grabbed her by the shoulders. "Feya left me because of you."

"Get your fucking hands off her." Jett was on his feet in seconds.

Before she even knew what happened, he slammed Shamus against the wall. He actually lifted Shamus' body off the floor. Jett held him there with his forearm against his chest. Shamus' feet dangled an inch from her welcome mat.

"You can throw sucker punches at me all day long. I don't give a fuck. But don't you ever lay your hands on a woman." Jett took a step back, letting Shamus fall to the floor.

He nearly toppled over.

Jett wiped his bloody lip.

"Get the fuck out of my home before I physically remove you." Jett opened the door. "You are not welcome here and don't contact me or my girl again. If you do, you'll regret it."

"Are you threatening me?"

Jett took a step forward.

Shamus took one toward the door.

"I'm not the kind of man you want to fuck with." Jett cocked his head. "Just ask your hopefully soon-to-be ex-wife what I did when one of her friend's exes got handsy with her and you'll understand why." He gave Shamus a shove and slammed the door. He leaned against the structure, closed his eyes, and let out a long breath. "I'm sorry."

"For what?" Winslet raced to his side, palming his face. She couldn't imagine what Jett was apologizing for. Yeah, he was a little aggressive, but fuck, Shamus came in hot. Real hot. The situation was volatile, and she was scared. Her hands were still freaking shaking. "The jerk hit you. In your apartment. All you did was confirm what his wife thought. You didn't do anything wrong but defend both of us."

"I'm glad you see it that way." He blinked open his eyes. "You haven't seen this side of me. I do have a temper. Especially when it comes to that kind of shit. I can take a fist sandwich. I'll walk away from chest pounding and pissing contests. But I struggle with men who either strike a woman or put their paws on them when they don't want them to. It's a hot button for me."

"Are you the kind of man who will stop what you're doing when you see an injustice wherever you are?"

He nodded.

"Chuck's that way too. One of the many reasons I like that man so much." She wrapped her arms around

Jett and held on for dear life. “Did something happen to make you like that? Because for Chuck, there’s a story.”

“No story, really. I just have a little sister who’s pretty as hell. A few times guys would whistle at her and say gross stuff and I’d tell them to back off. But nothing ever happened.”

“Your sister’s lucky to have you.”

“I’m the lucky one.” He tipped her chin. “I’m also pretty lucky that you’re in my life. Now, don’t we have a list of pros and cons to make?”

“Can you still be impartial?”

“Nope.”

She laughed. “At least you’re honest.”

# CHAPTER FIFTEEN

"How are you holding up?" Jett leaned against the kitchen counter. Last night's events were still fresh, raw, and totally shocking.

Shamus had emailed the university to inform them that he was withdrawing from his guest lecture due to a family emergency.

Good riddance.

Feya had texted Jett, stating that she intended to file for divorce, but she wanted to make it as gentle as possible for her children. She didn't know what that looked like, but she needed the support of her family to do that. He told her to reach out to his sister and the rest of the old gang.

They would be there for her.

He and Winslet would be too, but that would be weird, for both women.

However, the hardest part of last night had been the fact he was ready to say those three little words, but fucking Shamus came in and ruined the night. Of course, Jett had a few more opportunities to utter words of love, but he couldn't bring himself to do it.

He told himself it was too soon. Or that he'd gotten caught up in a sweet moment. Whatever the reason. He'd backpedaled.

"I can't believe Weston and Haven questioned my dad on and off for six hours." She sat at the kitchen table, hunched over her coffee. "But it's his and Cooper's behavior that has me baffled. Cooper's coming hard after my dad. Even accusing him of killing my grandfather. Weston said he was screaming at him at the station to tell everyone where he buried the body. I don't understand."

"Weston and I were chatting about this while you were in the shower." Jett pulled back a chair, flipped it around, and straddled it. "Cooper's adamant that Hannah wasn't having an affair with your grandfather. The only rumbling he's willing to give any merit to is the one between your grandma and your great-uncle, but he won't say anything other than it's a big fat rumor."

"You're rambling and it's annoying." She tilted her head and shot a dozen daggers from her sweet eyes.

"The four of them were best friends." Jett inhaled sharply, letting it out with a swoosh. "According to the research that Weston did, Hannah was desperate to have a child. That she and Cooper had been trying for five years, but nothing. Fertility wasn't the same back then and options were limited."

"Would you please get to the point."

"Hannah had a miscarriage a month before she disappeared."

"I didn't know that."

"I guess she and Cooper kept it quiet," Jett said. "Weston has asked for her medical records. It might shed some light on this."

"I don't see how."

"Cooper admitted that some of their fertility problems were because of a low mobility rate on his part. It wasn't impossible for him to get his wife pregnant, but it wasn't a high probability without medical help." Jett waved his finger. "He admitted to borrowing money from your grandfather for treatments."

"Interesting that this never came up before."

"Cooper didn't see the relevance. He's never believed that your grandfather had an affair with Hannah. Or that they ran off together. He's always maintained they were murdered."

"By my father."

Jett nodded. No point in denying that fact.

*Knock. Knock.*

"Who the hell could that be this early?" Jett rose and made his way to the front door. He pulled back the door. "Mr. Payne? What are you doing here?"

"Where's my daughter? I need to talk to her." Winslet's father sidestepped Jett.

While Thomas' eyes were bloodshot, they were also wide-open and wild with anger. His hair was disheveled. He paced in the small foyer. "Is she here?"

"Daddy?" Winslet appeared in family room. "What's going on?"

"This is a goddamn shit show." Thomas planted his hands on his hips.

That's when Jett noticed the weapon tucked in the back of his pants.

Shit, that wasn't good. Jett's gun was locked up in a cupboard in the kitchen.

Why the hell was Thomas packing?

Jett ran his fingers through his hair. He needed to defuse the situation. He needed to get the upper hand of whatever Thomas had planned. He needed his cell.

And he needed his fucking weapon.

Not necessarily in that order.

WINSLET STARED AT HER FATHER. He'd always been a well put together man no matter what was going on in his life. He never let the rumor mill control his actions, which had been obvious to her growing up because of all his affairs. He never seemed to care what anyone thought.

Whenever people whispered about the murders,

he'd tell his girls that unsolved crimes just made people gossip about stuff they had no idea about. He'd tell them that someday the truth would come out. That his parents' killer would be brought to justice.

That the crime would be solved, and they would all be allowed to live in peace.

And if it didn't, not to let the chatter bother them because it didn't matter. He knew the truth.

"I don't know who Weston thinks he is or why Chief Hill is allowing this to happen. It's fucking ridiculous," her father said.

"What are you talking about?" Winslet asked.

"Weston's at the house right now with a search warrant. I don't know what he thinks he'll find, but it's police harassment." Her father had fire coming from his eyes. She'd never seen so much rage before. Her dad had always been a mild-mannered kind of person. He almost never raised his voice.

That had always made it hard for her to hate him. He wasn't violent. Or mean. He never belittled his children. Although he did play favorites between his two daughters, which she'd made easy by being the *bad* child. Even though he cheated on his wife, which was disrespectful, he showered her mother with affection when they were together.

As if to make up for his lying ass.

"Where's Mom?" Winslet inched closer to Jett. She needed to feel his presence. His kindness.

His love.

Jett wrapped his arm around her waist.

"She spent the night at Tammy's," her father said. "I texted her and told her to spend the day there. But I didn't tell her what was going on. I don't want this to touch her. Considering everything, this is the last thing she needs."

"What does that mean?" Winslet blinked. Her mind rolled her father's words around, but nothing made sense.

Her dad pointed his finger in her face. "You just had to stick your nose where it didn't belong. First, by telling your mother about what you saw all those years ago. Then poisoning your sister against me. Now she's filling your mother's head full of ideas." He poked her in the chest.

Jett stepped between them. "Don't you dare touch her again."

"Fuck off. This doesn't concern you," her dad said. The smell of whiskey tumbled from his breath like the ocean breeze rolling onto the shore.

Her dad wasn't a big drinker. At least not that she ever saw.

"Your mother thinks she wants to leave me." Her dad took a step back. "I'm not going to let that happen. Just like I'm not going to prison for something I didn't do." He shook his head violently. "I did not kill my mother. I watched my dad pull the trigger."

Winslet covered her mouth and gasped.

"If that's the case," Jett said calmly. "Why didn't you

tell the police at the time?" He held Winslet tight. His arms were like a warm blanket on a cold winter night.

She grappled with the revelation, trying to make sense of it. A million questions flooded her brain, but she couldn't open her mouth to ask a single one.

Her dad tossed his head back and laughed. It wasn't a funny laugh. More like a menacing, murderous laugh.

"Oh my God," Winslet whispered. "You killed Grandpa, didn't you?"

"Was it in self-defense?" Gently, Jett pushed Winslet behind him. "I'm sure all this can be explained away. Why don't we call Weston. He's a reasonable man. You were a teenager who witnessed a traumatic event and—"

"They will twist it." Her father reached into his jeans and pulled out a gun.

"Jesus, Dad. What the hell?" She clutched Jett's shoulders.

"I'm not going to prison. I can't. Not after all these years." Her dad waved his gun around like a lunatic before he pointed it directly at Jett's chest. "You're good friends with Weston and his wife. I need you to tell them they're wrong. Tell them something about those bones you found. Tell them anything. I don't care. Just get them out of my house and off my back so I can fix things with my wife and go about my life."

"There's nothing to tell," she said softly. "Bones don't lie and there wasn't much information they gave us other than who she was. That she was originally buried somewhere in Fallport, and she was shot twice in the chest with… oh shit." Winslet swallowed.

"What?" Jett glanced over his shoulder.

"The ballistics on the bullets I found in her chest must have come back and it had to have matched my grandfather's gun," she said.

"We have to spin that, so it was my dad who killed her." Her father narrowed his stare. "My father. He killed Hannah. She showed up when he was trying to clean up the mess."

"Why was Hannah at the house?" Winslet asked, her voice finally gaining strength. She tried to inch around Jett, but he wouldn't let her. Not that she wanted a gun pointed anywhere near her body. However, she didn't like it aimed at her boyfriend's heart.

"I'd like the answer to that and to why your father killed your mom as well," Jett said. "Why don't you put that thing away and we can sit down and talk this through and figure out a plan."

She dug her nails into Jett's shoulders. What fucking plan? There was only one thing to do. Call the cops and have her father taken in. Even she could see that. Regardless of the outcome, he needed to tell the story to Weston. Or Haven. Or Chief Hill. If he was justified—as in self-defense—when it came to her grandfather, she'd accept that.

But she was struggling to understand why Hannah Wilks had to die.

"No." Her dad held the weapon steady. Not bad for

a drunk man. Or maybe he was just hungover. "My daughter here is going to call Weston and give him a logical explanation of why they are barking up the wrong tree. She will get them out of my house and off my property. My father is still missing. They need to be searching for him. He killed my mother. Therefore, he killed Hannah. It's that simple."

Just like that, a lightbulb went off in Winslet's brain. "Okay. I'll help you, but only if you tell us everything that happened. I need the truth. If I don't have that, I can't develop a plausible misdirection in this case."

"That sounds like a bunch of bullshit to me." Her dad cocked a brow.

"You think I want to see my dad go to prison?" she said. "I might hate how you cheat on Mom. Actually, I think you're a snake for doing that. I know how that feels. It sucks. But that doesn't change the fact you're still my dad and I love you." All that was true. She loved her father. With all that she was. It would probably never change. Even though she was staring at a cold-blooded murderer.

Maybe he was somewhat justified for killing his father.

But she couldn't imagine he was when it came to Hannah.

Slowly, her father lowered his weapon. "That, I actually believe."

"Put that thing away and I'll go make some coffee." Jett let out a long breath. He held his palm out.

"I'll keep this close." Her dad lowered his chin. "Just in case."

Now all Winslet needed to do was get the truth, turn on her father, and not become another casualty in the insanity of her past.

# CHAPTER SIXTEEN

The last thing Jett wanted to do was leave Winslet in the family room with her dad and a loaded gun. But he needed his weapon and his cell. It was the only way. He sent off a quick text to Weston and Haven, letting them know the situation, copying Zeke and the gang. Then he went about making coffee, snagging a few bagels, and making sure his weapon was loaded and tucked in his ankle holster before returning to the family room where Thomas sat on the recliner, his gun in his lap. Winslet was on the sofa with her feet curled up under her butt.

He placed the tray on the coffee table as if this were a normal morning with his girlfriend's father.

There was nothing normal about this.

"Shall we start from the beginning?" He lifted his coffee, blew into the steaming mug, and took a slow sip, letting it burn the roof of his mouth. For whatever reason, it needed to do that. It reminded him he was alive.

He'd hoped this move—this job—would mean no more bullets flying in his direction.

No more near-death experiences.

He planned on that last one to hold true.

But he sure as shit would step between Thomas and Winslet if he had to. No way would he let anything happen to the woman he loved.

How crazy was that?

"It's a simple story, really," her dad said in a monotone voice, void of emotion.

Damn, was that how he sounded when he spoke of his past? If it was, he totally understood why people thought he was way too pragmatic about things. He had a shit ton of feelings swirling around in his soul about his life. His past relationships. His life events. His logical brain was his way to deal with the pain.

Dumb way to do that.

"People in this town have forgotten what a mean man my dad could be," her father said. "Even Cooper knew what a jerk my dad could be, but they were friends, and he wants to only remember the good times. Not the times he would rage on my mother." Thomas waved his weapon in the air. "My mom was no saint. She started having an affair with my dad's brother when I was ten. Maybe even younger. I'm not sure. But that's when I learned about it."

Jett wanted to say that the apple didn't fall far from the tree, but he knew better. It wouldn't help the situation, and it would only serve to make Winslet feel worse about what happened with Shamus.

"I'm sorry, Dad," Winslet said. "But you getting upset over your mom having an affair is hypocritical."

Thomas pulled his lips into a hard line. "I honestly didn't care. I sure as hell didn't tell my father. I didn't want them to get divorced and neither did my dad. He wanted them to stay a family. He even told my mom she could fuck whoever she wanted as long as they were discreet and no one knew. But my mom wanted to run off with Uncle Xavier. They planned the whole thing and what I didn't know was that Hannah Wilks was going to help her."

"So, this is why you've hated your uncle all these years," Winslet said.

Her dad nodded.

"Did you ever confront Xavier about it?"

"No," her father said. "He was a sad and pathetic loser. He acted like he cared about my father's disappearance. He cried over it even. But really, the only thing he cared about was my mother being dead and the fact he was stuck with me."

"Did he suspect you?" Jett asked.

"I have no idea. When I turned eighteen, I moved out." Her dad shrugged. "Until he started to lose his mind, we stayed clear of each other."

"Did Cooper know all this?" Jett asked.

"I don't think so, because if he did, he would have told the police. But that's why Hannah showed up that morning. I had already disposed of my father's body and was getting ready to deal with my mom when Hannah came bouncing into the kitchen, ready to help my mother with her exit strategy. Whatever the fuck that meant."

"Jesus," Winslet muttered. "I need to know what you saw. Grandma was shot in the back. Why did Grandpa do that? And why did you kill Grandpa?"

"Does it matter?" Her father jumped to his feet.

"Yes," Winslet said. "Motive matters. If I'm going to redirect, I need all the information."

Jett had heard enough. He didn't need any more information. What he needed was the cavalry.

But he wouldn't deny Winslet her answers.

However, the gun being waved frantically about the apartment made him more than nervous. Thomas was a fucking loose cannon. He killed once before, and he'd do it again. Especially when backed in a corner.

Jett didn't need to be a cop to know that.

"My folks were fighting about Uncle Xavier. I could hear them. I came downstairs because I was tired of it. I told them to shut up." Thomas swiped at his eyes with his free hand. Tears rolled down his cheeks. "My dad's gun was in the corner by the door. I picked it up. I yelled at them to get their shit together. I told them I didn't care about any of it. All I wanted was a family.

My mother tried to explain that we could be a family even if my parents weren't married. My dad said he'd never give her a divorce. That one of them would have to be dead for their marriage to end. My mother looked him square in the eye and told him it was over. She was leaving and there was nothing he could do about it." Thomas paced in front of the coffee table. He pointed the gun between Jett and Winslet. His eyes turned from gut-wrenching sadness to rage in a split second.

Jett eased from the sofa. He knew that what Thomas had stated earlier had been a lie.

Marcus hadn't killed Lola.

Thomas wanted that to be the truth. Perhaps he'd buried that so deep in his psyche that for all these years he believed it. But now he had no choice but to face the reality.

"My mom turned her back on us. She fucking turned around as if we weren't even standing there. It was like we didn't even matter. Like she didn't even care we existed." Thomas paused. He held his weapon steady. Aimed right for Winslet. "My dad looked at me as I raised the rifle. He came toward me. I think he said something as he reached for the gun. It went off. Twice. He shot her in the back. She crumpled to the ground. I was so stunned. I looked down. My fingers were still gripping the cold metal. He accused me of doing it. But he was coming for the rifle. I was trying to stop him from taking it and killing her. It was all his fault. I raised it and shot him once in the center of his chest. That's all it took." Thomas sighed. "Hannah showed up hours later. I had no choice. I'm sorry about that." He narrowed his stare, jaunting his weapon forward. "Now you know the sordid truth. Make it go away. Help me end this and talk your mother out of leaving me. We're a family. No matter what, we belong together. You may not understand this, but I love your mom. She's my world."

"You have a funny way of showing it," Winslet whispered.

"You don't know what you're talking about." Thomas gripped the handle with two hands. "I've given your mother everything and she's going to leave me now? I don't think so. Call Weston. Tell him it would be impossible for me to have killed any of them. Do it, or this ends badly for both of you."

"Do not threaten her. Or me for that matter." Jett reached for his gun strapped to his ankle.

*Bang.*

Fuck.

A searing pain tore through his shoulder. He jerked back, stumbling to the sofa, landing on top of Winslet.

She screamed.

The sound of the front door cracking open—no, more like being knocked down—shattered his ears.

"Drop your weapon," Weston's voice rang out.

"Don't move," Haven said, inching closer. "We've got this building surrounded."

"You're under arrest." Weston plucked the gun from Thomas' hand and pushed him to the ground.

Jett blinked. His arm went numb. But his shoulder felt as though something had severed it from his body. A little dramatic, and it wasn't true, but that didn't change the pain registering in his brain.

Winslet pressed her hand on the wound. "He fucking shot you."

"Tell me something I don't know," he managed through labored breaths. "This is my good shoulder too. Well, it's better than the other one in the sense that I've less surgeries on it."

"Please don't make jokes." Winslet leaned over and kissed his forehead. "Although, at least it was your shoulder and not your chest."

"Yeah. That's looking at the bright side of things." He winced as she put more pressure on his shoulder. He glanced down. Blood trickled through her fingers. Damn, that was a lot of blood. He heard more voices in the background.

Zeke maybe. Definitely Tal and his buddy Lincoln. Those two were easy to pick out of a crowd because of their British accents.

"What the hell, man," Zeke said, standing over him. "Why am I always sitting at your bedside after you get shot?"

"At least this one isn't life or death." His tongue stuck to the roof of his mouth. "I think."

"You've been through worse." Zeke squeezed his good shoulder. "I'm going to help Weston with a few things, and then I'll see you shortly."

"Thanks." Jett gave Zeke a weak smile.

"You're going to be fine." Winslet palmed his cheek.

"I'm sorry."

She narrowed her eyes. "For what?"

"For getting shot. For not being able to be with you for the next few hours, or maybe even the next day or two to deal with the fallout of this." His eyes burned. "Maybe I should have tried to disarm him—"

"Stop that." She kissed his lips. "We didn't know he'd go off. He's my father and I had no idea."

"Ma'am. We need to get an IV going on him and transport him to the hospital," someone said.

"Oh fun. I get the good drugs," he whispered.

"Yes, sir. You do," the EMT said. "Some real good stuff."

"Can I ride with him?" Winslet asked.

"Sure thing. But once I give him some pain meds, he's going to be real loopy," the EMT said.

"You're making a mistake," Thomas yelled. "This was all a misunderstanding. I didn't mean for the gun to go off."

Jett rolled his head. What a horrible day for Winslet. So much pain. She'd been through so much and to add this to it all? It had to be too much for her. She would for sure bolt out of this town as fast as she could. He let out a long breath. He couldn't blame her for that. He'd probably do the same thing.

His mind raced with a million things.

He loved her.

He should follow her wherever she went.

Yeah. That's what he should do. He loved Fallport. But he loved her more.

# CHAPTER SEVENTEEN

Winslet sat at the small table in the waiting room with Weston. It had been four hours since they wheeled Jett into surgery. Deep down, she knew Jett was going to be just fine. They needed to get in, get the bullet out, and assess the damage. But at the end of the day, he wasn't going to die.

"You need to know we found remains in your father's backyard. State called in another forensic anthropologist," Weston said. "You're too close to this one."

"Yeah. I'll agree with you on that one." She swallowed.

"I interviewed your dad. He admitted to me that the body buried in his backyard is his father, but we have to go through the motions."

"Jesus." Her stomach twisted and churned. Bile filled her throat. "We've lived in two homes since I was born. Did he bring his dad with him wherever he went?"

Weston nodded. "He moved Hannah about fifteen years ago. But he felt like he needed to keep his dad close. I know that's weird and feels like a trophy, but he's not a serial killer."

"But he is a murderer."

"He signed a confession. He's using a public defender, which is fine, but it's almost like he's given up. Resigned to the fact he'll most likely spend the rest of his life in prison." Weston took her hands. "I wish we got to Jett's place sooner."

Her mom and sister came barreling through the doors. "Winslet." Her mother yanked her from the chair and hugged her so tight she could barely breathe. "I'm so sorry. I've been so worried about you."

"I'm fine. It's Jett who got shot," she mumbled as tears streamed down her cheeks.

"I can't believe all this is happening. That your father… my husband… I'm… I… I just don't… Oh my God… What are we going to do?"

The impact of her mother's words slapped her heart like a runaway train. She held her mom while she sobbed in her arms. Her poor mother's world had flipped on its head.

"Mom, it's going to be okay." She stroked her mother's hair. "You didn't do anything wrong. Dad did and no one in this town is going to hold you responsible for his actions."

"I've been living with... living with... a monster." Her mother hiccupped.

Winslet cupped her mom's face and stared into her bloodshot eyes. "Don't go blaming yourself for something you can't control. You didn't know. None of us did. Not even the cops. And they have been looking for years. All we can do now is pick up the pieces of our lives, hold our heads high, and keep living." Damn, there was something to Jett's way of thinking. To his pragmatic way of life.

She still needed to go through all the grief. All the emotions. All the feelings of what was to come. And she knew it would be hell.

But living her life would be the best medicine.

"I don't know how I'm going to be able to even leave my house," her mother whispered.

"Mom." Tammy wrapped her arm around their mother's shoulders. "We have each other. We'll be okay no matter what."

A doctor appeared in the doorway.

Winslet turned, squeezing her mother's hand. "Is Jett out of surgery?"

"Yes." The doctor nodded. "Everything went well. The bullet landed in some scar tissue. We removed it, cleaned everything up, and Jett will be as good as new in no time. It's amazing what that man has endured in his life. While this wasn't a life-threatening injury, Jett is damn lucky to be alive."

"Can I see him?" Winslet asked.

"He's doped up, so he's feeling mighty good right about now. But he's asking for you," the doctor said.

"We'll leave you to visit your boyfriend." Her mother gave her a big hug.

"No. I don't want you to leave." She took her mom by the forearms. "We all need to heal, and we need each other. I need you. I want you to stay. Both you and Tammy. That is if you want to."

"Of course I do." Her mom kissed her cheek. "I love you girls so much."

"I love you too." Things were far from good with her family. But she was going to make damn sure that she had a decent relationship with her sister.

And her mother.

This dark cloud that lived over their heads for decades was going to disperse. It would take time. But Fallport had seen its fair share of scandal. The Payne girls were strong. They would get through this.

And she would find a way to have Jett in her life.

* * *

JETT DESPERATELY WANTED to push the pain med button. But he knew the second he did that, he'd be higher than a kite and probably half-asleep.

Or more than likely, completely passed out for a good hour.

He knew the drill.

Been there. Done that.

Too many fucking times.

The curtain swung open.

Thank God.

He smiled. "Boy, are you a sight for sore eyes."

Winslet sat on the edge of the bed and took his hand. "This better be the last time you take a bullet—for anyone."

He chuckled. "I can get down with that plan." He reached up with his good arm and wiped a tear from her cheek. "Why are you crying?"

"I just saw my mom. She's a hot mess. She's so worried about what everyone in this town is going to think of her. Of us."

"And what about you?"

She cocked her head. "I used to always worry about that. I hated how my father was openly cheating on my mom. Or the rumors about my grandfather. But now that the truth is out there—for everyone to judge—I seem less concerned. People have an opinion of me. They are going to whisper about what happened. But eventually, it will die down. Another scandal will happen. I mean, look at Haven. She went through hell when she came back to this town. But no one ever talks about that anymore."

"You're starting to sound like me now."

"I'm beginning to think there's something to your pragmatic approach to life."

He took her hand and kissed the palm. "As long as

you don't go and do what I've done and stuff those emotions so deep you don't feel them."

She arched a brow. "What does that mean?"

"While your dad was waving his gun around, mostly pointing at you. And then in here waiting for you to come see me. I've had some time to ponder my life."

"Should I be scared?"

"Maybe." He was utterly terrified she was going to go running out of the room and disappear from his life forever. "When we first met, you accused me of what most women have. Being emotionless. And you wouldn't be completely wrong. While I feel like everyone else does, I don't allow those emotions to linger. Especially painful ones." He pressed his finger over her lips when she opened her mouth. "For example. When Kiki left me. I was honestly devastated. I did love her. I won't deny that. Same with Becky. But I stuffed that pain. I chose to ignore it. I chose not to fight. And I chose to close myself off. I won't do that again. I love you. I know it's fast. I certainly know you're dealing with a lot. However, I want to be the guy who helps you through it all. I don't care if it's here in Fallport or somewhere else. Geography doesn't matter. What does matter is that we do it together." He spoke so fast that he could barely understand the words that tumbled out of his mouth. Jeez, he hoped he made sense.

"Are you trying to tell me you'd quit your job and follow me if I decided not to take the professorship?"

Her lashes fluttered fast and furious over her big, beautiful eyes.

"Yes. Because I love you. I want to be with you. I want to create a life with you. I want a future with you and I won't let you walk out of my life without putting up a fight."

"You couldn't take me right now if you tried." She wiped away the tears and smiled.

He rolled his eyes and sighed. "Are you seriously not going to respond to the fact that I've said I love you now three times?"

"You're totally drugged. I want to hear you say it when you're not in this hospital bed or on any pain meds."

"That's kicking a man when he's down."

She leaned over and kissed him tenderly. "The doctor said he's releasing you tomorrow. If you want me to nurse you back to health, that's the way it's going to be."

"You drive a hard bargain." He raised the button that would release more of the good stuff into his system. "I'm going to hit this and I'll be asleep in a matter of seconds."

"I'll be here when you wake up," she whispered. "I'm not going anywhere."

"Good to know." He tapped it. Warmth filled his veins. A numbness came over his body. He stared into her loving eyes. Whatever this woman wanted, he'd give it to her.

He'd been searching for Winslet his whole life. She was his soul. His heart. His world.

"Sleep," she said.

His eyelids grew heavy.

"I do love you, Jett."

Or at least that's what he thought he heard her say as he drifted off into a blissful dream state where the world made sense and Winslet would always love him.

## CHAPTER EIGHTEEN

"You have to be the worst patient known to man." Winslet set a tray of food on the bed and climbed in. "You're so demanding."

Jett laughed. "You're the one who told me not to get out of bed. I think I can manage to make my own sandwich." He lifted the BLT from the plate and took a hearty bite. It had been a week since he'd been shot.

In those seven days a lot had happened.

Her father had been shot and killed when he tried to escape during transport.

That had been sad and horrific, driving the point home as to what he'd done.

Her mother was currently living with Tammy and wanted to put the family home up for sale.

That was understandable.

But through it all, Tammy, Winslet, and their mom had grown closer. They talked every day. It was tough sometimes. Painful. So much hurt from so many years of misunderstandings and words that could never be taken back. However, they were committed to their healing process.

They had even decided to go to counseling together.

Winslet owed it to her family not to do what she did best.

Run.

She'd done that when Harvey cheated on her and she felt the weight of her family's transgression come down on her shoulders. It was as if she couldn't come back because of the rumors swirling around about her grandparents.

Her father.

Her ex-fiancé.

But that hadn't been the case.

It was the shame she felt of being betrayed. The worry of being judged for something she hadn't done. For something that she didn't control.

All she'd wanted to do was pretend it didn't happen, and she thought leaving was her only choice.

She knew better this time.

She snuggled in next to him, stealing a couple of his potato chips. "I don't think I've ever said—thank you."

"For what?" He jerked his head.

"For everything. For being there for me. Taking a bullet for me." She took the sandwich out of his hand, set it on the plate, and pushed it to the side. "For loving me."

"All things that you don't need to thank me for." He lifted her chin with his thumb. "But I wouldn't mind hearing something else."

"I've said it already." She smiled.

"Maybe, but I was half sleeping and drugged. I'm wide awake and not on a single painkiller." He waggled his brows. "So, what's it going to be? Are you going to break my heart? Or tell me what I know you feel in your heart?"

"You're an impossible man." She kissed his forehead. Then his temple. Then his sweet lips. "I love you. It's crazy. But I'm head over heels, madly, deeply in love with you." She covered his mouth. "But I don't want you to quit your job. If you were still in the military, I wouldn't ask you to leave."

"I don't have to give up being a park ranger. I can do that somewhere else. I'm also a certified EMT. I have skills that can be utilized anywhere. You're not asking me to give up my job. We're simply talking about where I'm going to put what I do to use." He lowered his chin. "Just like I'm not going to ask you to give up your passions. You have a career to—"

"Oh my God. Be quiet for just one second." She let out a big puff of air. "I'm going to accept the professorship at the university here. I don't want to leave my mom and sister. And for the record, I'm not doing that out of obligation. I'm doing it because the three of us need each other if we're going to come out of this shit show that my father created on the other side. I also have Emory and Oliver to consider. Again, not making this decision solely because of them." Winslet had never felt so good about a decision in her entire life. For the first time, she knew she was exactly where she needed to be. "I was lost when I first came back to Fallport. I was floundering in self-pity. Maybe even a little self-hatred. Then you found me. But you didn't save me. You just showed me a path out. And you loved me. Isn't that what being partners is all about?"

"Come here." He curled his fingers behind her neck and pressed his mouth against hers in a passionate kiss. "I love you. Now can I finish my lunch? I'm starving."

"Only if I can eat half your chips." She placed the plate back on his lap. "Oh, and don't get mad, but my sister is feeling a little crowded with my mom over there all the time. But my mom will not go back to the family home, and I don't blame her for that. So, I told her she could come to my apartment anytime she wanted." She tilted her head, plopping a chip between her lips.

"That's reasonable." He winked. "Does that mean you're never leaving my bed? Because I'd be really lonely if you did. I mean, I can't do anything with this arm in a sling. I can't even fasten my own jeans."

"You're pathetic. Five minutes ago… Yeah. It means you're stuck with me." She sighed. "I love you, Jett McCoy."

"Right back at you, Winslet Payne."

# EPILOGUE

## TWO MONTHS LATER...

Jett fiddled with his wedding ring as he stared at his bride chatting with his parents and grandma. It had been a bigger wedding than he'd wanted. It had started out with just his family, Tammy and her broad, and Winslet's mom. But there were too many people in Fallport he couldn't leave out. Zeke and all the guys at Search and Rescue.

Weston and Haven.

Chuck and Renee.

Zeke had served as his best man. Tammy as the matron of honor.

And Chuck officiated the wedding, which turned out to be quite humorous.

"Hey, big brother." Evelynn plopped herself on the barstool.

Holding a wedding reception at On The Rocks was an interesting venue choice, but Zeke insisted. And it was free, so who was he to argue. Besides, Zeke had been so many things to Jett and his family. No way would Jett say no.

"Hey, yourself," Jett said. "Having a good time?"

"Hell yeah." She lifted her wineglass and tapped it against his tumbler. "How the heck did you luck out with the likes of Winslet? She's amazing."

"I keep pinching myself, wondering when I'm going to wake up."

"Don't fuck this one up."

He laughed. "I won't. She won't let me."

"Good, because I'm keeping her." Just then one of Evelynn's kids came running across the bar, yelling something about what his older brother had done. "Shit. I better go find out what that's all about since his father is too busy hanging on Chuck." She smacked her forehead. "Does everyone have a man crush on that one?"

"I wouldn't kick him out of bed."

"Ew. Gross." Evelynn slipped from the barstool and chased off after her kids.

Jett caught Winslet's gaze as she strolled across the room in her wedding dress. It wasn't a traditional dress, although it was white. It was strapless, came to her knees in the front, and hung at her ankles in the back.

Oddly, she wore white sparkly tennis sneakers.

Whatever made the woman happy.

He couldn't have cared less. If she wanted to wear

jeans, he would have been fine with that. He just wished she didn't make him wear a freaking suit and tie. That he could have lived without.

"Hi, husband." She smiled.

"You like saying that, don't you?"

She nodded, setting her water on the bar.

"Still not feeling well?" She'd woken the last few days with a sour belly.

He chalked it up to nerves. Meeting his family right before the wedding hadn't been ideal. But she had been called to work a crime with the FBI. His sister had classes and couldn't come down.

Things were hectic.

And his family could be a lot. Well-meaning. Kind. Generous. Loving. But ballbusters. The entire lot of them.

"I'm fine." She leaned in and kissed his scruffy face.

At least she didn't ask him to shave. He'd grown accustomed to his new beard.

"Then how about a glass of wine or champagne to celebrate?" He checked his watch. "We've been married now for over an hour."

"Are you counting the minutes because you're feeling like I'm the old ball and chain?"

"Never." He jumped from the stool and eased between her legs, nuzzling his face in her neck, kissing the tender spot right under her ear. "I'm literally the happiest man in this room."

"I don't know. Chuck's pretty giddy about making everyone laugh at our wedding. At your expense."

"I'll get him back for telling the story about how I fell off the ATV into a pile of mud and nearly lost the ring trying to propose to you."

"I doubt that," she whispered. "I believe he's got something else in store for you." She cupped his face as Chuck clanked his glass.

"Can I have everyone's attention, please," Chuck said into a microphone.

"What's he doing now?" Jett looped his arm around Winslet and braced himself for God only knew. Chuck had an arsenal of funny stories on everyone in this room.

Winslet included.

But he'd told all the good ones already on Jett, so he had no idea what this guy had up his sleeve.

Winslet shrugged.

"Winslet asked me to put together this little presentation for everyone," Chuck said, pointing to a computer and then to Zeke, who was putting up a screen.

"Sweetheart, what have you done?"

"Just watch, honey," she cooed, kissing his neck. A single tear dribbled down her cheek. She swiped it with a delicate finger.

"I had to reach out to Jett's family for some baby pictures," Chuck said.

Jett groaned. "Sweet Jesus. This is going to be embarrassing."

"Hey, there's some of me too." She pointed to the screen as one appeared of her and her sister in some big bathtub. They were covered in bubbles and had taken markers or something and rubbed it all over the walls. And themselves.

More images of their respective childhoods flashed on the screen.

And then of them together.

It was honestly very sweet. It touched his soul in ways he didn't expect. Winslet was his wife. No. She was his partner in life. His soulmate.

"This is the first picture of Winslet and Jett as man and wife," Chuck said proudly. "And let's all congratulate them as they embark on this new journey." The image on the screen changed.

It was black and white. No. More black and gray. It looked like a blob.

He'd seen this before, though his brain couldn't remember where, or what it meant.

"Raise your glasses," Chuck said. "To Jett and Winslet and their new family."

His breath left his lungs in one big swish. His heart jumped to his throat.

Everyone in the room erupted in cheers. His mother screamed something about being a grandma again.

But he wasn't sure of her exact words because he was sure he had wax in his ears.

Winslet wrapped her arms around his shoulders. "I know we talked about this for like in a year, but I guess this is what happens when I go off birth control and we aren't always careful about—"

"I know how babies are made." He cupped her face. Tears burned his eyes. But at least they were happy ones. "I love you and this is the best news ever." He kissed her hard. He didn't care that half the room surrounded them, and this was definitely the kind of kiss that should be done in private. "I can't believe you told Chuck before you told me."

"That's a funny story." She pointed across the room. "Look."

He tilted his head and laughed. Hard. "Well, shit. Renee's pregnant too?"

"The only reason I told Chuck was because Renee and I took the tests together. They weren't even trying. They were done. But when he caught us, I had to let the cat out of the bag, so Renee could surprise him, and this is what we came up with."

He dropped his forehead to hers, wiping the tears from her cheeks. "You are going to be a fantastic mom. I can only hope I'll be as good a dad."

"Are you kidding?" She smiled so wide he fell in love with her all over again. "I wouldn't have let you knock me up if I didn't know you'd be the best."

Jett had finally found home.

. . .

Thank you for taking the time to read *Searching for Winslet.* Please feel free to leave an honest review. Grab a glass of vino, kick back, relax, and let the romance roll in...

*Sign up for my Newsletter (https://dl.bookfunnel.com/82gm8b9k4y) where I often give away free books before publication.*

*Join my private Facebook group (https://www.facebook.com/groups/191706547909047/) where I post exclusive excerpts and discuss all things murder and love!*

# ABOUT THE AUTHOR

Jen Talty is the *USA Today* Bestselling Author of Contemporary Romance, Romantic Suspense, and Paranormal Romance. In the fall of 2020, her short story was selected and featured in a 1001 Dark Nights Anthology.

Regardless of the genre, her goal is to take you on a ride that will leave you floating under the sun with warmth in your heart. She writes stories about broken heroes and heroines who aren't necessarily looking for romance, but in the end, they find the kind of love books are written about :).

She first started writing while carting her kids to one hockey rink after the other, averaging 170 games per year between 3 kids in 2 countries and 5 states. Her first book, IN TWO WEEKS was originally published in 2007. In 2010 she helped form a publishing company (Cool Gus Publishing) with *NY Times* Bestselling Author Bob Mayer where she ran the technical side of the business through 2016.

Jen is currently enjoying the next phase of her life…the empty nester! She and her husband reside in Jupiter, Florida.

Grab a glass of vino, kick back, relax, and let the romance roll in…

*Sign up for my Newsletter (https://dl.bookfunnel.com/82gm8b9k4y) where I often give away free books before publication.*

*Join my private Facebook group (https://www.facebook.com/groups/191706547909047/) where I post exclusive excerpts and discuss all things murder and love!*

Never miss a new release. Follow me on Amazon:amazon.com/author/jentalty
And on Bookbub: bookbub.com/authors/jen-talty

# ALSO BY JEN TALTY

***Fallport Rescue Operations***

***Searching for Madison***

***Searching for Haven***

***Searching for Pandora***

***Searching for Stormi***

***Searching for Winslet***

***Hawaii Brotherhood Protectors***

***Waylen Unleashed***

***Bowie's Battle***

***Brand new series: SAFE HARBOR!***

***Mine To Keep***

***Mine To Save***

***Mine To Protect***

***Mine to Hold***

***Mine to Love***

***Check out LOVE IN THE ADIRONDACKS!***

***Shattered Dreams***

***An Inconvenient Flame***

***The Wedding Driver***

*Clear Blue Sky*

*Blue Moon*

*Before the Storm*

**NY STATE TROOPER SERIES (also set in the Adirondacks!)**

*In Two Weeks*

*Dark Water*

*Deadly Secrets*

*Murder in Paradise Bay*

*To Protect His own*

*Deadly Seduction*

*When A Stranger Calls*

*His Deadly Past*

*The Corkscrew Killer*

***First Responders: A spin-off from the NY State Troopers series***

*Playing With Fire*

*Private Conversation*

*The Right Groom*

*After The Fire*

*Caught In The Flames*

*Chasing The Fire*

***Legacy Series***

*Dark Legacy*

*Legacy of Lies*

*Secret Legacy*

**Emerald City**

*Investigate Away*

*Sail Away*

*Fly Away*

*Flirt Away*

**Colorado Brotherhood Protectors**

*Fighting For Esme*

*Defending Raven*

*Fay's Six*

*Darius' Promise*

**Yellowstone Brotherhood Protectors**

*Guarding Payton*

*Wyatt's Mission*

*Corbin's Mission*

**Candlewood Falls**

*Rivers Edge*

*The Buried Secret*

*Its In His Kiss*

*Lips Of An Angel*

*Kisses Sweeter than Wine*

***A Little Bit Whiskey***

***It's all in the Whiskey***

***Johnnie Walker***

***Georgia Moon***

***Jack Daniels***

***Jim Beam***

***Whiskey Sour***

***Whiskey Cobbler***

***Whiskey Smash***

***Irish Whiskey***

***The Monroes***

***Color Me Yours***

***Color Me Smart***

***Color Me Free***

***Color Me Lucky***

***Color Me Ice***

***Color Me Home***

***Search and Rescue***

***Protecting Ainsley***

***Protecting Clover***

***Protecting Olympia***

***Protecting Freedom***

***Protecting Princess***

*Protecting Marlowe*

**DELTA FORCE-NEXT GENERATION**

*Shielding Jolene*

*Shielding Aalyiah*

*Shielding Laine*

*Shielding Talullah*

*Shielding Maribel*

*Shielding Daisy*

**The Men of Thief Lake**

*Rekindled*

*Destiny's Dream*

**Federal Investigators**

*Jane Doe's Return*

*The Butterfly Murders*

**THE AEGIS NETWORK**

**The Sarich Brother**

*The Lighthouse*

*Her Last Hope*

*The Last Flight*

*The Return Home*

*The Matriarch*

**Aegis Network: Jacksonville Division**

*A SEAL's Honor*

*Talon's Honor*

*Arthur's Honor*

*Rex's Honor*

*Kent's Honor*

*Buddy's Honor*

*Aegis Network Short Stories*

*Max & Milian*

*A Christmas Miracle*

*Spinning Wheels*

*Holiday's Vacation*

*The Brotherhood Protectors*

*Out of the Wild*

*Rough Justice*

*Rough Around The Edges*

*Rough Ride*

*Rough Edge*

*Rough Beauty*

*The Brotherhood Protectors*

*The Saving Series*

*Saving Love*

*Saving Magnolia*

*Saving Leather*

***Hot Hunks***

***Cove's Blind Date Blows Up***

***My Everyday Hero – Ledger***

***Tempting Tavor***

***Malachi's Mystic Assignment***

***Needing Neor***

***Holiday Romances***

***A Christmas Getaway***

***Alaskan Christmas***

***Whispers***

***Christmas In The Sand***

***Heroes & Heroines on the Field***

***Taking A Risk***

***Tee Time***

***A New Dawn***

***The Blind Date***

***Spring Fling***

***Summers Gone***

***Winter Wedding***

***The Awakening***

***Fated Moons***

***The Collective Order***

*The Lost Sister*

*The Lost Soldier*

*The Lost Soul*

*The Lost Connection*

*The New Order*

*There are many more books in this fan fiction world than listed here, for an up-to-date list go to www.AcesPress.com*

*You can also visit our Amazon page at: http://www.amazon.com/author/operationalpha*

***Special Forces: Operation Alpha World***

Christie Adams: Charity's Heart
Elizabella Baker: Challenging Luke
Linzi Baxter: Dangerous Rescue
Misha Blake: Flash
Anna Blakely: Rescuing Gracelynn
Julia Bright: Saving Lorelei
Cara Carnes: Protecting Mari
Kendra Mei Chailyn: Beast
Melissa Kay Clarke: Rescuing Annabeth
Gia Cobie: Saved from Revenge
Samantha Cole: Handling Haven
KaLyn Cooper: Spring Unveiled
Jordan Dane: Redemption for Avery
D.M. Earl: Claire's Guardian
Riley Edwards: Protecting Olivia
Dorothy Ewels: Knight's Queen
Lila Ferrari: Protecting Joy
Nicole Flockton: Protecting Maria
Amy Gamet: Guarded by the SEAL
Lea Griffith: Finding Ava
Desiree Holt: Protecting Maddie

Danielle M. Haas: Crossroads of Betrayal
Bree Hera: Trusting the Team
Jesse Jacobson: Protecting Honor
Rayne Lewis: Justice for Mary
Ireland Lorelei: The Detective
Kristin Lynn: Worth the Risk
JM Madden: Rescuing Olivia
A.M. Mahler: Griffin
Ellie Masters: Sybil's Protector
Trish McCallan: Hero Under Fire
Naomi McKay: Twist
KD Michaels: Saving Laura
Olivia Michaels: Protecting Harper
Annie Miller: Securing Willow
MJ Nightingale: Protecting Beauty
C.K. O'Connor: Delaney's Bodyguard
Melinda Owens: Betraying Katie
Victoria Paige: Reclaiming Izabel
Danielle Pays: Defending Sarina
Lainey Reese: Protecting New York
KeKe Renée: Protecting Bria
Taryn Rivers: Savage Cove
TL Reeve and Michele Ryan: Extracting Mateo
Ariana Rose: Chasing Paige
Angela Rush: Charlotte
E.M. Shue: Discovering Tyler
Rose Smith: Saving Satin
Tyler Anne Snell: Cowboy Heat
Dee Stewart: Fighting for Brielle

Lynne St. James: SEAL's Spitfire
Bella Stone: Rexar
Jen Talty: Protecting Ainsley
Reina Torres, Rescuing Hi'ilani
LJ Vickery: Circus Comes to Town
R. C. Wynne: Shadows Renewed

***Delta Team Three Series***

Lori Ryan: Nori's Delta
Becca Jameson: Destiny's Delta
Lynne St James, Gwen's Delta
Elle James: Ivy's Delta
Riley Edwards: Hope's Delta

***Police and Fire: Operation Alpha World***

Freya Barker: Burning for Autumn
B.P. Beth: Scott
Jane Blythe: Salvaging Marigold
Julia Bright: Justice for Amber
Gia Cobie: Saved from Revenge
Hadley Finn: Exton
Danielle M. Haas: Crossroads of Betrayal
Deanndra Hall: Shelter for Sharla
Jenna Harte: Dead But Not Forgotten
India Kells: Game Master
Amber Kuhlman: Protecting Paisley
Reina Torres: Justice for Sloane
Aubree Valentine, Justice for Danielle

***Tarpley VFD Series***

Silver James, Fighting for Elena
Deanndra Hall, Fighting for Carly
Haven Rose, Fighting for Calliope
MJ Nightingale, Fighting for Jemma
TL Reeve, Fighting for Brittney
Nicole Flockton, Fighting for Nadia

***As you know, this book included at least one character from Susan Stoker's books. To check out more, see below.***

**SEAL of Protection: Alliance Series**

*Protecting Remi*
*Protecting Wren*
*Protecting Josie (Mar 4, 2025)*
*Protecting Maggie (Apr 1, 2025)*
*Protecting Addison (May 6, 2025)*
*Protecting Kelli (TBA)*
*Protecting Bree (TBA)*

**The Refuge Series**

*Deserving Alaska*
*Deserving Henley*
*Deserving Reese*
*Deserving Cora*
*Deserving Lara*
*Deserving Maisy*
*Deserving Ryleigh (Jan 7, 2025)*

**SEAL Team Hawaii Series**

*Finding Elodie*
*Finding Lexie*
*Finding Kenna*
*Finding Monica*
*Finding Carly*

*Finding Ashlyn*
*Finding Jodelle*

**Eagle Point Search & Rescue**

*Searching for Lilly*
*Searching for Elsie*
*Searching for Bristol*
*Searching for Caryn*
*Searching for Finley*
*Searching for Heather*
*Searching for Khloe*

**Delta Team Two Series**

*Shielding Gillian*
*Shielding Kinley*
*Shielding Aspen*
*Shielding Jayme (novella)*
*Shielding Riley*
*Shielding Devyn*
*Shielding Ember*
*Shielding Sierra*

**SEAL of Protection: Legacy Series**

*Securing Caite (FREE!)*
*Securing Brenae (novella)*
*Securing Sidney*
*Securing Piper*
*Securing Zoey*

*Securing Avery*
*Securing Kalee*
*Securing Jane*

**Delta Force Heroes Series**
*Rescuing Rayne (FREE!)*
*Rescuing Aimee (novella)*
*Rescuing Emily*
*Rescuing Harley*
*Marrying Emily (novella)*
*Rescuing Kassie*
*Rescuing Bryn*
*Rescuing Casey*
*Rescuing Sadie (novella)*
*Rescuing Wendy*
*Rescuing Mary*
*Rescuing Macie (novella)*
*Rescuing Annie*

**Badge of Honor: Texas Heroes Series**
*Justice for Mackenzie (FREE!)*
*Justice for Mickie*
*Justice for Corrie*
*Justice for Laine (novella)*
*Shelter for Elizabeth*
*Justice for Boone*
*Shelter for Adeline*
*Shelter for Sophie*

*Justice for Erin*
*Justice for Milena*
*Shelter for Blythe*
*Justice for Hope*
*Shelter for Quinn*
*Shelter for Koren*
*Shelter for Penelope*

**SEAL of Protection Series**

*Protecting Caroline (FREE!)*
*Protecting Alabama*
*Protecting Fiona*
*Marrying Caroline (novella)*
*Protecting Summer*
*Protecting Cheyenne*
*Protecting Jessyka*
*Protecting Julie (novella)*
*Protecting Melody*
*Protecting the Future*
*Protecting Kiera (novella)*
*Protecting Alabama's Kids (novella)*
*Protecting Dakota*

*New York Times, USA Today* and *Wall Street Journal* Bestselling Author Susan Stoker has a heart as big as the state of Tennessee where she lives, but this all American girl has also spent the last fourteen years living in Missouri, California, Colorado, Indiana, and

Texas. She's married to a retired Army man who now gets to follow *her* around the country.

www.stokeraces.com
www.AcesPress.com
susan@stokeraces.com

Made in United States
Cleveland, OH
23 June 2025